# LAST DITCH

## *A WWII Action Thriller*

## John Wingate

SAPERE
BOOKS

# LAST DITCH

Published by Sapere Books.

20 Windermere Drive, Leeds, England, LS17 7UZ,
United Kingdom

saperebooks.com

ISBN: 978-1-80055-345-3

*The British people, secure in their islands, take for granted these days of peace, yet only yesterday (speaking historically) Britain alone remained, after the collapse of Europe, to face the Nazi onslaught.*

*Only a narrow stretch of water divided Britain from the enemy, and day and night, winter and summer, the battle for the Channel was waged.*

*This is the story of the gruelling tasks and the heroism of the men in the little ships: motor torpedo boats, gun boats, destroyers, balloon ships.*

*Among the many thrilling, often tragic and moving, scenes of action are the evacuation from Dunkirk, the relentless shelling of convoys of merchant ships in 'the graveyard' and the disastrous raid on Dieppe.*

*All the descriptions of action are historically accurate, based on the records and on the personal stories of survivors whom the author knows.*

# ACKNOWLEDGEMENTS

I wish especially to express my thanks to Rear Admiral P. N. Buckley, C.B., D.S.O. and to his preessor in office, Lieutenant-Commander P. K. Kemp, O.B.E., both Heads of the Naval Historical Branch who, with their staffs, have spared no pains and given me every encouragement; and to Lieutenant-Colonel W. B. R. Neave-Hill for his kindness and help as Head of the Army Historical Branch.

For their patient co-operation and their generosity, I am deeply indebted to Vice-Admiral J. Hughes-Hallett, C.B., D.S.O.; Captain Peter Loasby, D.S.C., R.N.; Captain Peter Dickens, D.S.O., M.B.E., D.S.C., R.N. (Ret'd); A. R. H. Nye, Esq., D.S.C.; J. H. Coste, Esq., D.S.C.; Norman Ffitch Esq.; Air-Commodore J. Constable-Roberts; Captain G. Blundell, C.B.E., R.N. (Ret'd); Captain R. N. MacDonald, C.B.E., R.N.; Captain E. N. Pumphrey, D.S.O., D.S.C., R.N. (Ret'd); Lieutenant-Commander W. Willett, O.B.E., D.S.C., M.I.L., R.N. (Ret'd); Captain Garth Owles, D.S.O., D.S.C., R.N. (Ret'd); Alan Forster Esq., M.B.E., Tony Puckle Esq., M.B.E., John Meade, Esq., L. H. Blaxell, Esq., D.S.C.; Captain I. A. B. Quarrie, C.B.E., V.R.D., D.L., R.N.R.; Mr T. Keegan; Paul Boyle Esq.; H. Daniel Hall Esq.; M.I.MechE.; Mr G. W. Dolan; Mr J. P. Hupfield; Mr J. B. Baldwin; Mr K. G. Stone, D.S.M.; Mr B. G. Cook; Mrs W. Puttick; Mr A. S. Sturtevant; Mr R. Popple; Mr E.D. Houghton; Mr F. S. R. Bowen.

Full acknowledgement and my thanks are also due to G. D. Blackwood, Esq., of William Blackwood and Sons, Ltd, for permission to include in chapters 5 and 6 the late Lieutenant R.

G. Addis's story, A *Channel Passage* which was published in November 1942 in Blackwood's Magazine, Number 1525, Volume 252. I am also deeply indebted to the family of Lieutenant Addis who have graciously consented to the use of his article.

I am also indebted to Peter Scott, C.B.E., D.S.C., LL.D., for his kindness in allowing me to quote passages from his narratives on Coastal Forces which he recorded so vividly in his book, *The Battle of the Narrow Seas.*

Finally my sincere gratitude is due to Admiral of the Fleet, the Earl Mountbatten of Burma, K.G., P.C., G.C.B., G.C.S.I., G.C.I.E., G.C.V.O., D.S.O. for his encouragement and for allowing me to quote his address to the people of France and to the Allies at the Commemoration of the Twenty-fifth Anniversary of the Dieppe Raid on 19th August 1942.

*10 Downing Street, Whitehall*
*30th May, 1943.*

*I have noted with admiration the work of the light coastal forces in the North Sea, in the Channel and, more recently in the Mediterranean. Both in offence and defence the fighting zeal and the professional skill of officers and men have maintained the great tradition built up by many generations of British seamen.*

*As our strategy becomes more strongly offensive, the task allotted to the coastal forces will increase in importance, and the area of their operations will widen.*

*I wish to express my heartfelt congratulations to you all on what you have done in the past, and complete confidence that you will maintain the same high standards until complete victory has been gained over all our enemies.*

WINSTON CHURCHILL

# FOREWORD

It is impossible to thank adequately all those who have made this book possible. So many have helped, so much information has been freely given. My main regret is that, owing to the necessity of keeping the narrative to a reasonable length, I have been unable to include all the accounts which I have been privileged to receive from those who participated in this ruthless Battle of the Narrow Seas.

Sub-Lieutenant Bruce and Third Officer Suzanne Noyce, W.R.N.S., are the only main fictional characters. Through the episodes which they experience, episodes based on accumulated and factual evidence, the reader shares the events of those three climacteric years and lives alongside the valiant men whose deeds are recorded herein.

Not only did these little ships combat the Germans, night in, night out for five years: the sea itself was the unconquerable adversary, with its swiftly-shifting moods, its menace and its venom. This undulating mass of water, with its gales, its fogs and its swingeing tidal streams, this English Channel was the real enemy, common to both friend and foe.

And what of the men? Whence did they come? They were you and me, ordinary Britons, culled from their shop floors, their work benches and their offices; from their farmsteads and garages. Some met their death within a fortnight of joining their first little ships; some, like Nigel Pumphrey and Peter Dickens, miraculously survived those five long years.

And do these restless seas, still sweeping back and forth over the graves of those who lie in peace below, make us wonder if the merciless struggle was futile? Did the adversaries pour out the blood of their young manhood in vain?

I think not.

Not if those who were spared still hold fast; not if those who remain continue with resolution the eternal struggle for the Christian decencies for which the forces of freedom died.

'See that ye hold fast the heritage we leave you, yea and teach your children its value, that never in the coming centimes their hearts may fail them or their hands grow weak.'

These words of Sir Francis Drake are inscribed in the stone of the Chapel of Remembrance at the Britannia Royal Naval College, Dartmouth.

# CHAPTER 1

*The nine days' wonder:*
*26th May — 4th June 1940*

The young man stood motionless for a moment outside the bustling entrance to Dover station. His gas mask was slung over his right shoulder and from his left hand drooped the grip which contained his emergency personal gear. *Sub-Lieutenant W. Bruce, R.N.* was stencilled in black upon the khaki canvas of his holdall, but apart from this identification, there was little to distinguish him from any of the scurrying figures dispersing into the gloom of this wartime twilight. The wail of the all-clear from the siren was dying away, and for an instant there was peace, save for the crying of the gulls as they flew lazily inland for the night.

Walter Bruce took off his cap to feel the wind in his thick fair hair; he was weary from the long journey from Glasgow where he had left his ship. With only half an hour's warning, he had been ordered south to report to Headquarters at Dover. He had been informed that because he had gained his watch-keeping certificate, he could be useful in the Dover command, but otherwise he was told nothing. Yet, during the long journey southwards, the rumours of disaster multiplied: the Belgians were surrendering to the Germans, now that Holland was overrun; the French armies were in full retreat; with its back to the sea, the British Expeditionary Force had been cut off and was fighting for its life while Hitler's Panzers closed in from all sides.

Wally Bruce's eyes, as blue and clear as the waters of the Moray Firth whence his forbears came, looked upwards to the castle which towered, proud and defiant, high above Dover town. The battlements were silhouetted against the lowering clouds, a sky which reflected the last blood-red streaks of another sunset. In this silence, Wally felt an intense foreboding, a realisation that events of gigantic proportions were about to unfold. This awareness emphasised the atmosphere of crisis that seemed to be Dover. He shook himself, smoothed his hair and replaced his cap.

'D'you want the castle, sir?' a husky voice asked quietly. 'There's a truck leaving now.' The Chief Petty Officer, part of the Rail Transport Officer's team, indicated a 15-cwt Bedford which, jammed with personnel, was waiting at the kerb, its darkened lights casting an oval pool of dim blue light upon the road.

'Thanks, Chief.'

Wally scrambled into the front seat. The C.P.O. saluted and banged shut the door of the truck. Wally was alone with his thoughts as the Bedford whined its way up to the castle. *Things will never be the same again for me*, he thought. *All my training during these long years will soon be put to the test.*

'Who are you?'

The questioner was the skipper of the drifter *Comfort*, a sturdy boat who had spent her peacetime days fishing off the banks of the Thames estuary. A rugged, unshaven seaman looked up with bleary eyes through the wheelhouse window at the young Lieutenant standing on the quay, a group of sailors at his back in the darkness.

'Sub-Lieutenant Bruce, sir. We've come to help with the boatwork.'

The skipper shrugged his shoulders and grunted, and then came the sound of the wheelhouse door opening. 'Ye better come aboard.'

The two men shook hands in the darkness. The skipper pointed towards the for'd hatch. 'Ye'd better kip down below for a wee bit. Ye'll be needing your sleep.'

Ten minutes later the little drifter, *Comfort,* slipped unnoticed from Dover south-west quay. She moved across the black waters of the harbour, then, to the throb of her heavy Gardiner diesel, she chugged between the breakwaters to set course for the open sea. The swell suddenly took her as she slid into the cross tide.

'What course do I want?' the skipper grunted.

Wally was still crouched over the chart which, cocoa-stained and crumpled, was spread out in the diminutive cubbyhole on the port side of the wheelhouse. A pool of blue light illuminated the ancient chart.

'Is the chart up to date, Skipper?'

'Up to last Friday, yes. I can't keep up with the corrections,' the old man grumbled, 'now that there's a new swept channel every other day.'

Wally smiled in the darkness. This independent Scotsman was, for once, adhering to the swept channels. The thumping diesel would certainly detonate any acoustic mines within reach.

'I'll take route Z,' the skipper growled. 'It's only thirty-nine miles compared with route Y.'

'You're ordered to use route Y, Skipper,' Wally said quietly. 'The Calais batteries have made Z pretty hot.'

The skipper spun the wheel to port as he sighted the South Foreland buoy flashing on his port bow.

'It's just as hot this side, Subbie. The Luftwaffe even shoots up our lightships now. The South Foreland has been replaced by that buoy. Can ye see it?'

'Yes, Skipper.'

'Take your departure from there, then. I'll use route Z: they won't see us in this darkness and we'll be there before dawn.'

'Aye, aye, Skipper.' Wally ran his parallel ruler over the chart, his stomach heaving with the combination of fear and the drifter's uneasy motion. Like all seamen, he detested the magnetic mine. The sudden, blinding flash in the darkness, the roar, and then the deluge of water; he hadn't experienced this new warfare yet. Scapa Flow and the relative safety of a cruiser in the North Sea off Norway had been comparatively peaceful, in spite of the vicissitudes of that heart-rending campaign.

'Course for Calais buoy, route Z, south seventy east,' Wally reported.

The skipper grunted. The wheel spun again. The drifter heeled, then settled down on her new course.

'Another fine night,' Skipper Craig said. 'This'll be your first trip, then?'

'To Dunkirk?'

'Yes,' Craig growled. *Dunkirk.*'

Wally resented the contemptuous note in the man's voice.

'It's a ruddy shambles, getting those bomb-happy troops off.'

In the silence, Wally heard only the swish of the water as *Comfort* dipped into the cross swell. He watched the granite features of the Scottish skipper, the craggy face that gleamed in the glow of the binnacle.

'Angus, ye take her. Course, south seventy east.'

A cadaverous figure detached itself from the corner of the wheelhouse and, without a word, took over the steering. Skipper Craig moved alongside Wally. The old Scot removed his cap and extracted from it his foul pipe. He filled the bowl with some evil-smelling tobacco, then applied the slow-match that hung from below the chart table. Clouds of smoke filled the tiny wheelhouse, and Wally suppressed the choking cough that threatened to overwhelm him: he wanted the dour Scot to continue the conversation.

The frequency of the pipe-sucking decreased, and then — peering through the open windows of the dog-house, at 2330 during the night of Monday, 28th May 1940 — the old Scot began to talk in the darkness, as is the custom of seamen during the long watches of the night.

'The weather's been like this since the evacuation started,' growled Craig. 'Ruddy miracle if you ask me. A mill pond off the beaches, except for once or twice; ruddy miracle, Subbie, that's what it is.'

'What's it like, Skipper? Off the beaches?'

Craig did not speak at first. Wally logged the South Foreland light, then returned to the binnacle. A running fix had put them half a mile south of the line.

'Could you come round to south seventy-five east, sir, please?'

'Bring her round, as the subbie says, Angus. Course, south seventy-five east.'

'South seventy-five east, Skipper. Aye, aye.' Wally heard the soft voice of the Western Islander. Angus and Craig had worked together, it seemed, for many years.

'If the weather had been bad, Subbie, we wouldn't have got off more than a few thousand. We move into the shallows as far as we dare, load up and ferry them off to the destroyers. When they're full up, I take on as many as I can and return to Dover.'

'Easy as kiss-your-hand,' Angus said. 'Except for them Stukas.'

No one spoke for a long time. Wally had not yet been dive-bombed: the Junkers JU 87s — or Stukas, as they were being called — could not reach Scapa or the Norwegian fiords.

'What's my E.T.A... Dyck Buoy, Subbie?'

'0320, at 10 knots, Skipper.'

Craig nodded. The skipper broke the long silence, but he expressed the thoughts in all their minds as they passed three sweepers, inward bound, their dimmed minesweeping lights just visible in the darkness.

'They've got guts,' Craig said, 'them sweeper boys.'

'Don't much like these magnetics,' Angus murmured. 'Ye never know.'

'D'you think we'll beat this menace, Subbie?' the skipper asked, almost childlike. 'The Hun has got us by the throat this time: most of the ports are closed.'

Wally hesitated: he had heard only yesterday that stocks of food were down to ten days throughout the country. All the ports were mined and the casualty rate of ships and sweepers was terrifying.

'We'll *have to* master this magnetic mine, Skipper, or we'll ruddy well starve.'

'What about this chap they're all talking about, then?' Craig asked. 'Bloomin' 'ero, I call 'im.'

'Ouvry, you mean? Lieutenant-Commander Ouvry?'

'Yes, that's the one. He's the chap who took a magnetic mine to bits in the mud off Shoeburyness. An aircraft had dropped it.' For this act, Ouvry had been awarded the D.S.O. for bravery.

'Didn't he describe every move he made to his mate on the other end of the telephone? In case he was blown up, like?'

'Yes,' Wally said quietly. 'I met Ouvry at *Vernon,* the Torpedo and Mining School. He was a quiet man.'

Craig was silent as, in the darkness, every man's imagination conjured up Ouvry's heroism.

Wally peered ahead into the blackness, but the sheen of the drifter's bow wave was the only glimmer of light. Drowsiness was beginning to engulf him, his eyelids aching from the strain of trying to keep awake.

A yellow flash of light leapt suddenly on their port bow. There was a rumble, a violent crack, and then an intense violet and orange flame.

'Not far off,' Craig snapped. 'Port ten, full ahead.' He picked up his binoculars and swept the horizon line where, in the darkness, the source of the flames must be. 'E-boats or some lurking U-boat,' Craig growled. The E-boats were the German equivalent of the British M.T.B. motor boats. 'Some poor blighter's bought it.'

*Comfort's* diesels were thumping at full speed, her hull quivering from the added power as she lifted to the swell.

'My God, Skipper,' Angus whispered, 'look at yon ship.'

He pointed with outstretched arm through the wheelhouse window, which the skipper had lowered. Wally tried to drag his eyes away, but the horror of the scene riveted his gaze upon the sea. Sticking up like two sore thumbs were the fore and after ends of a destroyer, her back broken. From amidships bubbled up gobs of black smoke where her boiler rooms were still exploding. Above the rending of the tortured metal wailed the shouts of trapped and drowning men. The bows and stern of the ship hung there, slowly dipping up and down in the swell like macabre marionettes.

'Look, sir...' Angus pointed to where a wedge of black heads bobbed in the oily sea, which gleamed fitfully from the flames of the burning ship.

The skipper took over the wheel and nursed his little drifter alongside the group of bedraggled swimmers. All hands had appeared from below, and soon the dazed survivors were being hauled over the drifter's bulwarks. Blankets were wrapped around the shivering men who, cigarettes now thrust between their lips, were gently escorted below into the saloon. Wally was hauling the last, an older man, from the water as Craig went full ahead to pick up the next knot of men struggling in the sea.

'I'm the captain,' the man gasped as, covered in slimy black oil fuel, he stumbled for'd on the slippery deck.

'What ship, sir?' Wally asked.

'Sorry, you wouldn't know, of course. I'm Commander Fisher,' the Captain said quietly. *Wakeful,* an old V and W destroyer. Torpedoed on the port side, amidships. U-boat probably, or could have been an E-boat — never saw the swine.'

Commander Fisher choked with emotion, shock overcoming his self-control. Wally put his arm around him and turned him gently round to retrace his steps.

'Come with me, sir, to meet Skipper Craig. You'll be warm in the wheelhouse.'

By the glow of the binnacle, Wally watched Craig, his skill tested to the utmost as he coaxed the little drifter to the next survivor, a man screaming and waving off the port bow.

'Captain of *Wakeful*, Skipper,' Wally said.

'Glad to have you aboard, sir,' replied Craig, not taking his eyes from the water. 'Sit ye down and Angus'll give ye a cuppa.'

'Thanks, Skipper. You arrived just in time,' Fisher said quietly.

'Och, all in the day's work. How long have you been doing the Dunkirk run?'

'Must be four days.' The Captain scratched his hair, matted by the oil. 'What day is it now? I've lost all count of time.'

'Twenty-ninth of May, Tuesday,' Wally said. 'How long will we be able to keep this up, sir?'

'Till we run out of destroyers.'

The door of the wheelhouse opened. Angus's face was silhouetted against the glare of the burning oil, which was already being extinguished by the long swell.

*Wakeful's* bow jutted into the sky, her pendant number, H-88, showing plainly as her fore-end dipped slowly up and down in the Channel. The shouts of the trapped men and the screams of the dying floated across the water through the scuttles, which were too small to allow men to escape. Her stern, hinged amidships, cocked upwards to form the second arm of a large V.

Commander Fisher stared up at Wally, agony in his dark eyes. Wally felt sick as he stumbled from the wheelhouse for air.

'There's a ship coming up on the other side of her,' Angus was saying. 'She's flashing a blue light.'

Wally snatched up the signalling torch from the wheelhouse seat. He identified a Halcyon-class minesweeper by the dark shape that had loomed up in the darkness which — mercifully— was beginning to envelop them as the flames died down.

'*Gossamer,* Skipper. She's picking up survivors.'

Angus poked his head through the door.

'We're awfu' full, Skipper. They'll have to stay on the upper deck now.'

Craig grunted. 'We'll go on until her gunwales are awash, man. Carry on getting 'em aboard.'

Wally had discarded his reefer jacket; it was warm work hauling these pathetic remains aboard. He slung his Mae West life jacket to one side, regarded it for a moment, then donned it again. Commander Fisher had now joined him and was patching up, as best he could, his torn and bleeding men.

'Look you, sir,' Angus shouted. 'Two more ships.'

To starboard of *Gossamer,* the sleek lines of a destroyer loomed in the darkness. She was flashing to another, smaller outline.

'That's *Grafton,*' Fisher shouted. 'She'll get my men out if anyone can.'

Though visibility had begun to shut down, Wally could distinguish also the unmistakeable outline of one of the old coal-burners; with her single funnel and unbroken upper deck, this latest arrival must be one of the ancient Hunt minesweepers.

'*Grafton*'s stopped to lower a boat,' Fisher said. 'Wish she'd keep moving. She's asking for it with these U-boats and E-boats lurking about.' He had picked up the wheelhouse binoculars and was concentrating on the sweeper.

'I'm sure that's *Lydd,* the old minesweeper. I passed her less than an hour ago.' He looked across at Craig. 'Could we close *Grafton,* please, Skipper?' he asked. 'I'd like to hail her Captain to see if he could put a party aboard *Wakeful to* break into the mess decks through the upper deck.'

Craig waited for another man to be hauled inboard before going ahead.

'I'm going for'd, Skipper,' Wally said, 'to keep a lookout, now that visibility's shutting right down.'

He wove his way through the packed upper deck, the smell of smoke and oil sour in his nostrils. He looked across to where *Grafton* and *Lydd* had been. He strained his eyes, peering into the thickness of the night. There was the ghostly outline of *Wakeful,* the cries of the trapped men still a terrible accompaniment to the screeching of the rending metal. There, right ahead, loomed the trim outline of the destroyer *Grafton*. Wally's eyes swept across her silhouette, searching for *Lydd*.

A vivid light leapt suddenly, the horizon a sheet of flame, the night erupting into awful sound. Wally stood rooted to the deck, horror sweeping over him. *Grafton* wallowed there, a gigantic void gaping beneath her bridge, steam roaring from her boiler rooms as her safety valves lifted, white plumes drifting to leeward as the southerly wind freshened.

'God,' a man gasped, 'poor bastards...' His blackened face twitched as he wept unashamedly.

Wally turned as he heard Commander Fisher shouting from the drifter's wheelhouse: 'For God's sake, all of you, keep your eyes skinned for E-boats. *They can't be...*'

A hail of bullets and shell splinters suddenly crashed into the upper works of the little drifter. Craig's horrified face appeared for an instant at the door of the wheelhouse as he peered upwards at the silhouette of *Lydd*, who was now within a hundred yards, her guns flashing as fingers of green tracer curled towards the defenceless drifter.

Wally threw himself flat across the heaped bodies that had streamed up from the saloon below. He tried to clamber aft as *Grafton*'s 4.7s joined in, but the wounded and the dying, the decks slippery with blood, the little ship disintegrating beneath the murderous fire, made his progress impossible. He glanced aft to see Commander Fisher leaping from the wheelhouse. Disregarding the exploding world about him, he was holding up his hands as if to ward off some invisible blow, his face working grotesquely as he shouted towards *Lydd*, who was already committed to the final phase of the tragedy.

Wally spun round. There, less than thirty yards distant, towered the bows of *Lydd* as she bore down upon her supposed adversary. Her bow wave gleamed at her stem. Her seamen could be seen pointing from her fo'c'sle. They turned suddenly towards their bridge as they saw and heard Fisher shouting:

'We're British… We're British, you ruddy fools. WE'RE NOT E-BOATS…!'

The destroyer Captain's words were drowned by the crash as *Lydd*'s bows sliced through the drifter's wooden hull. Wally braced himself to meet the shock, felt his body go rigid as, paralysed by terror, he watched the bow of the sweeper towering above them for an instant. He held his breath, felt the drifter lurch and then roll over under them as the water came up to meet him.

He gasped from the sudden cold of the sea. He saw a black mass sweeping past him, white foam threshing in the darkness. *The propellers,* he thought. *Get away, for God's sake, get clear…* He kicked with all his might, his arms flailing as he strove feverishly to swim clear.

An excruciating pain stabbed his head, there was a blinding light, and he knew no more.

# CHAPTER 2

*The Beaches*

Wally's first recollection of consciousness was the intense cold and the suffocation against which he was struggling convulsively. Then, with a jerk, he came to himself: he was alone in the water and was choking from the seas, which had increased with the breeze.

'Thank God for my Mae West,' he muttered to himself. He turned his head round the full horizon and there, to his astonishment, the macabre remains of *Wakeful* still jutted from the water, less than half a mile distant.

Though his head ached from the blow he had suffered when *Lydd* had rammed them, he must have been unconscious for only a short time: the other ships had disappeared, but *Wakeful* was close and making the same leeway in this breeze as he was. The screams from the trapped men were less audible now, though an occasional cry of despair reached him where he floated in the chill of the early morning.

'My God, I'm lucky,' Wally muttered as he offered up a silent prayer of thankfulness. 'I wonder if I'm *Comfort*'s only survivor?' What a ghastly tragedy — the sweeper, *Lydd*, and *Grafton,* the destroyer, could not be blamed for wrong identification, because they would be extremely sensitive after *Grafton*'s torpedoing seconds previously. *Grafton* must have sunk; *Gossamer* and *Lydd,* the two small minesweepers, had evidently picked up the survivors but had been unable to free those trapped men whose weird cries were now driving him to despair. He clapped his hands across his ears, but then found that he could not float properly. He pulled himself together and then, to his astonishment, he saw bearing down upon him, less than three cables away, the port bow of another sweeper: she looked very similar to *Lydd*.

*Don't panic, Bruce — keep calm. She'll see you if you wait until the right moment to shout. She's stopped her engines to investigate* Wakeful; *she's still moving ahead under her own way... Now, she's less than a hundred yards off... she'll run you down if you don't watch out...*

He yelled in the darkness, screaming his lungs out: 'Help! Help! For God's sake, *help...*'

He didn't want to drown... was terrified of being carved up by propellers. He'd only been in this war a few months...

He heard familiar noises above him and then, before he realised what was happening, the slab side of another minesweeper was towering above him. He felt the thump of her engines, registered the shouts of men, then heard the poppling of the water as she drifted down on top of him.

"'Ere ye are, matey... get hold of this. *Sheldrake* will look after you... easy now...'

He grabbed the heaving line which splashed across him. A scrambling net was hanging over the side where a sailor clung in the netting, his hands outstretched. Wally felt a pair of strong arms around him; a bowline was fastened under his armpits, and then he was gently yanked from the sea.

Rough hands shepherded him gently towards the 'break' amidships. He was trembling uncontrollably from the cold and delayed shock. He heard a voice from the bridge above him; the Captain was calling to the gun's crew on the fo'c's'le, his words distinct in the night.

'I'm giving no orders,' he said, 'but if you open fire by accident, I'll say nothing about it.'

The silence was shattered by the first round from *Sheldrake's* 4-inch gun on the fo'c's'le. An orange flash burst on the for'd part of *Wakeful*, who was now at point-blank range. Another round, then the 3-inch on the quarterdeck joined in, both guns firing together in agonised haste to finish this terrible work of mercy.

Wally felt sick as the butchery continued; men who had been onlookers now turned their faces away. Tears were streaming down an older man's face; a young ordinary seaman was being sick over the guard rails. Then, with a sudden rush, *Wakeful's* bows slid beneath the sea. Her stern section hung for an instant, then plunged with a swirl.

The guns ceased. There was a stillness during which men turned from each other; no longer did the cries of agony drift across the water on the whisper of the wind.

The warmth of the ward room and the kindness of the steward soon restored Wally to normality. The First Lieutenant gave him a pair of grey trousers and the Sub lent him a sweater.

'Let me have it back,' the fair-haired Sub said. 'My girlfriend made it for me — it's comforts for the troops.'

Wally smiled. The streaks of dawn were lightening the eastern horizon as he reached the upper deck. The ship heeled to starboard and a red-and-white buoy swung down their starboard side. A tall figure in a duffle coat and seaboots came lurching by, hand on the lifeline as he stumbled for'd along the upper deck.

'Well, Bruce, better now?' the First Lieutenant asked.

'Yes, thank you — much. May I work my passage, though? I don't like being a passenger.'

'Yes, Sub. Take the second whaler. We'll be off La Panne by 0600. Go inshore and load up with troops.'

'Aye, aye, sir.'

The First Lieutenant was already hurrying on to his next duty and was scrambling up the bridge ladder to report to his Captain. Wally glanced at the second whaler, the long seaboat still griped-to in the port davits abaft the funnel and abreast the midship structure. All looked well, so he had time for breakfast.

The sun was well into the sky when the boats were finally called away. He stood on the upper deck for a moment while the seamen streamed by him to their quarters. He looked towards the beach and caught his breath, his mind unable to assimilate the enormity of the disaster.

The port of Dunkirk was now two miles to the south west, where a pall of black smoke was billowing slowly upwards in a gigantic mushroom cloud and drifting down-wind: the Shell oil tanks, either dive-bombed or deliberately destroyed by British forces. The lighthouse stood up prominently at the entrance to the port and inside the long breakwater which stretched far out to sea. Bombs were already cascading on to the town from the Junkers 88s circling unmolested over the port; the Stukas, however, were obviously being reserved for individual targets such as the evacuation ships assembling off the beaches to the east.

Wally held his breath. A stream of Stukas was tumbling from the sky and plummeting downwards upon the sprawling mass of troops waiting upon the sands off La Panne and Malo-les-Bains. As the bombs struck, the black mass of humanity wavered like a swarm of flies upon an attic roof in the winter. The beaches from La Panne to Malo were patched by vast phalanxes of troops, moving and swaying on the sands like cloud shadows sweeping across the fields.

'Stand clear of the guard rails!'

Wally barely heard the cry as he watched the two-funnelled destroyer, less than half a mile away, being dive-bombed by the Stukas. *Malcolm,* identifiable by her black funnel top, was flotilla leader with Captain Tom Halsey, R.N., as Captain 'D'. She was twisting and turning under full speed and rudder to dodge the bombs released by the Stukas at the last moment. She had been hit not long ago by one of the Junkers 87s, when twelve sailors had been killed.

'Let go the gripes.'

Wally wrenched his eyes from *Malcolm* and took charge of lowering the boat.

'Lower to the guard rails — man the boat.'

He looked up at the bridge, where the First Lieutenant was standing in the wings.

'Ready to lower, sir.'

'Lower to the waterline.'

Wally turned to the seamen on the staghorns. 'Lower away.'

The blocks squealed, the whaler's crew clung to the lifelines.

''vast lowering.'

Wally peered upwards again.

'*Slip!*' called the First Lieutenant.

Wally waited for the swell to come up to meet the whaler. The bowman and sternsheetman were holding up their hands by the Robinson's disengaging gear.

'Ready to slip.'

'Slip!' Wally ordered.

There was a crash and the whaler wallowed alongside. The crew swung the lifelines inboard; Wally grabbed the after one and shinned down to the boat.

'Bear off for'd... ship your oars. Give way together.'

So began the day's toil, a day of long, heart-breaking work, a day in which Wally got to know his whaler's crew better than he'd ever known men before.

'Watch your time, Stroke... one-*out*; two-*out*; three-*out*...'

The whaler pulled slowly in towards La Panne, where the breakers curled up the sandy beach that shelved gently to the dunes. There, amongst those trees which the high-level bombers were plastering, were General Gort's Headquarters. The British Army was fighting for its life as Gort pulled in its rearguards. Alexander, Brooke, Montgomery were there: names as yet unheard, but fighting for the existence of 400,000 of the British Army. If the lines of the rearguards' perimeter broke, the B.E.F. would be swept into the sea.

It took twenty minutes for the whaler to pull into the surf. Wally turned her bows-on to the sea and held water to allow her slowly and safely to touch the sand. He unshipped the rudder while his crew jumped over the gunwales to hold her square to the sea.

'Come on, man the boat!' he called to a file of troops snaking down to the water's edge, but his words were inaudible in the hubbub on the beach. Stukas were spiralling downwards, their wingtip sirens screaming as they dived, a spine-chilling morale-breaker if ever there was one. ME 109s were skimming along the beaches and firing at everything that moved. Spurts of sand and black smoke would leap into the air as the bombs sank into the sand before exploding. It was miraculous that so few soldiers were hit; they either flattened themselves as the bomb-whistle shrieked towards them, or shovelled out fox-holes in the sand where they could lie in relative safety.

'One at a time, mateys, or you'll swamp the boat,' called Curtis, the whaler's Cox'n. 'All aboard for the Blighty-line...'

A mixed bag closed in on the whaler: R.A.S.C., Pioneer Corps, soldiers from all regiments.

''Scuse me, sir...'

Wally looked down at the face peering up at him from the gunwale. The man had lost his tin hat, his hair was matted with grease and sand, and his face was grey with fatigue and two days' beard.

'My name's Dolan, sir; Corporal Dolan. I've driven from Dixmude with these 'ere wounded. I took 'em in to Dunkirk, sir, to put 'em aboard the 'ospital ship on the jetty.'

'Why didn't you load them there, then?' Wally snapped.

'Ship was 'it as we were getting aboard, sir. She blew up in our faces and sank alongside.' He shrugged his shoulders. 'Stuka.'

'All right,' Wally conceded. 'Bring 'em along.'

Dolan had organised a party of stretcher-bearers, a French Army Captain from the Chasseurs Alpins, with several *poilus* amongst them.

'...'eave ... *hup*...'

The first stretcher was passed head-high across the water by upstretched arms until its pathetic burden was gently lowered across the thwarts.

'Stand back,' Wally ordered quietly. 'Let the next stretcher through.'

The French Army Captain had reached the gunwale on the whaler's port quarter, a diminutive soldier by his side whose face, barely above water, was entirely smothered by the French tin helmet.

'Monsieur, *aidez-nous!*' the French Captain was shouting above the scream of a diving Stuka. Some dozen French soldiers, rifles above their heads, were waiting patiently for their Captain.

'Come on, then!' Wally shouted. 'Come aboard…'

Bullets were kicking up spurts of water around the whaler, which now was listing dangerously to starboard as the French *poilus* tried to scramble over the gunwales.

'Permission to carry on, sir?' Dolan shouted, a grin across his Cockney face.

Wally looked upwards. A gigantic black vulture was hurtling downwards upon him, growing grotesquely with every second that passed. The leading edges of the wings were spitting flame, and now, behind the visor of the cockpit, grinned the face of the German pilot.

When almost upon them, the Stuka pulled out, its two wheels whistling as it passed overhead. Then, deceptively slowly, the great black egg of its bomb toppled from its underbelly. Wally watched its parabolic curve, then realised suddenly that the enormity was streaking straight on top of them.

'Get down!' he called at the top of his lungs. He threw himself flat across the stretchers lying upon the thwarts. He heard the shriek of the bomb as it toppled across the whaler, saw its mass disappearing behind the starboard gunwale. There was a muffled explosion, a vicious shock under him, and then the whaler lifted bodily. The boat was swamped and, with her gunwales awash, those troops who were still alive in the blood-stained water lunged for the starboard gunwale. The added weight was too much for the stability of the boat and over she went, on her beam ends, her occupants sliding into the sea.

'Get clear!' Wally called. 'Save the stretchers!'

He felt the sand under his feet as he grabbed one end of a stretcher, a Frenchman on the other. The torso of the decapitated French Captain floated by, back uppermost. The small French soldier, face white and staring, was out of his depth and clawing at the hand-ropes of the capsized whaler. The soldier's helmet had fallen off, and from the bobbed hair beneath it, Wally distinguished the head of a young woman.

'Hold on, for God's sake,' he shouted at her. 'We'll soon right the boat.'

Already his boat's crew, miraculously untouched, were scrambling upon the upturned boat. The leading seaman was grabbing the hand-lines and, with two others, was bracing himself outwards to roll her back on to an even keel. Others soon joined him and, within minutes, the whaler wallowed the right way up again in the surf.

Wally, his arms collapsing beneath the weight of the stretcher, flopped his end of it back across the gunwale. The other stretcher case had been retrieved but the patient was, by the look of him, already dead.

'Wait... *attendez...*' Wally shouted in desperation as the motley collection of terrified men grabbed again at the lifelines. 'We'll bail out first and *then* man the boat. For God's sake wait, then we'll be all right.

They started bailing with anything they could find. The woman in the French soldier's uniform was joining in with the rest, helmets used as bailers.

'The boat's holed for'd, sir,' the leading seaman said quietly. 'An eighteen-inch gash.'

Wally was silent. They'd never bail her out. 'Keep 'em bailing,' he said. 'I'll get help.'

'Come on, you skrimshankers,' the leading hand yelled, grinning across his wind-beaten face. 'Bail like hell, you bleedin' perishers.'

Wally could now stand in the stern sheets. A quarter of a mile away was *Malcolm,* weaving and turning in the restricted waters. Her motor boat had seen the capsize and was frothing towards them.

'Come on, bail!' he yelled. 'We're being picked up...'

Fifteen minutes later *Malcolm*'s motor boat had picked up Wally's contingent. Under the charge of her First Lieutenant, the stove-in whaler had been towed back to *Malcolm* and then sunk when the extent of the damage had been sighted. This flotilla leader had stopped for a few moments to pick up survivors, but as soon as her motor boat was clear again, she immediately went ahead, twisting and turning to avoid the attention of the Stukas. The wounded were lifted down to the sick bay, where the Surgeon-Lieutenant took them under his care, for only flotilla leaders boasted the luxury of a surgeon.

'Well, Sub,' a Lieutenant greeted Wally by the torpedo tubes. 'I'm going up to the bridge. Would you like to see the Captain?'

Wally, water still oozing from his shoes, saluted and grinned. 'Thank you, sir. I'd better ask your Captain what's the best thing to do. I left *Sheldrake* not so long ago — if she's not missing me she'll be wanting her whaler.'

'Come on, then. I'm Ian Cox, acting First Lieutenant.' The Lieutenant led the way for'd to the break in the fo'c's'le, where he scuttled up the bridge ladder to the wings that led on to the bridge itself. At the voicepipe stood the sturdy figure of the Navigating Officer, Lieutenant David Mellis; in the corner the Captain sat rock-like on the bridge chair.

'Captain, sir,' Cox introduced. 'Sub-Lieutenant Bruce up to see you. He was in *Sheldrake*'s whaler when we picked her up.'

A square, craggy man turned towards Wally, a warm smile of welcome on his face, which was crumpled like a boxer's; an ugly face, full of humour and integrity. Five foot eight inches tall, yet as wide as a barn door, Captain Halsey looked as tough as a gnarled oak. 'Tom', as he was affectionately known by the ship's company — a ragtail of a crew, yet welded under Tom's command into a happy and efficient ship — demanded the best from everyone and usually obtained it. His wrinkled eyes smiled at Wally.

'Welcome to *Malcolm,* Sub,' he said, extending his hand. 'There's really not much time to send you back to *Sheldrake.* I'll signal her and tell her you're staying here with me. Any objections?'

'No, sir. Thank you.'

'Stukas, green four-o, sir,' shouted the starboard lookout, arm pointing up-sun. 'Angle of sight, eight-o.'

'Excuse me, Sub. I have to earn my bread and butter.' Captain Halsey moved quietly to the voicepipe. 'Full ahead both,' he ordered without raising his voice. 'Cox'n on the wheel.' He squinted upwards, then, never for an instant taking his eyes from the hovering group of five dive-bombers, he strode to the bridge side. 'Open fire,' he snapped. 'Hard-a-port.'

David Mellis, the flotilla's Navigating Officer, had dived for the chart table, whence he extracted his tin hat; Wally jumped to the back of the bridge to keep out of the way. Fascinated, he watched the process of being dive-bombed, his hand across his brow as he peered with half-shut eyes into the glare of the sun.

The Captain was wrenching the bows of *Malcolm* round until he judged the JU 87s to be right ahead. The ship, now trembling from her full power as she worked up to 27 knots, had little sea-room in which to manoeuvre. David Mellis had jumped on to the compass platform from where he conned the ship under the crisp orders from the Captain.

'Midships — meet her — *steady*. Stand by, David...' —
squinting upwards now and shielding his eyes from the sun —
'... now. Hard-a-starboard.'

*Malcolm* lunged outwards as she turned at full speed, her guns
blazing from all quarters: the five 4.7s could not elevate
enough yet but, in addition to her 3-inch H.A. gun, her two 2-
pounders, the 0.5-inch machine guns and four Lewis were
firing away merrily. Wally glanced downwards, along the iron
deck to where soldiers had added their unofficial armament: a
battery of Bren guns had been rigged up wherever a jury
mounting could be found — there was even an organised
firing squad on the after-control which, with its rifles, was
carrying out controlled volleys under the direction of a young
subaltern.

Then Wally became aware of a piercing, blood-chilling shriek
that overpowered even this cacophony of gunfire. The fiendish
noise swamped his mind, numbing all rational thought. He
looked upwards. The leading Stuka was less than eight hundred
yards above them, and hurtling downwards in a vertical dive.

'Hard-a-starboard,' the Captain ordered.

'Hard-a-starboard, sir,' repeated David Mellis, his eyes on the
compass card, chart in hand. 'We're reaching the edge of the
deep, sir.'

Tom Halsey nodded.

'Midships — meet her.'

He had driven right in under the Stuka, which, unless it
turned in on itself, would overshoot astern. Halsey grinned as
the black egg shot from the 87's midriff — down it hurtled, a
twisting enormity tumbling down on top of them. It grew to
hideous proportions, to plunge harmlessly into the sea off the
port quarter.

The crack of the explosion had not died away before the next 87 was on top of them. David Mellis was chuckling, his granite face tense, his rugged Scottish features wreathed in amusement.

'You've got 'em taped this time, sir!'

'"Make-ee learner," that one. Second eleven.'

Tom Halsey had succeeded in manoeuvring his ship right under the Stukas' dives. Their bombs fell astern, but near enough to drench all those on the upper deck. Yet, less than a mile away, *Gallant* had just been hit. She lay stopped with smoke and flames leaping from amidships.

When he had handed back the ship to the Officer of the Watch, Mellis came over to Wally. 'It's been a bad day,' he said. 'Too many casualties amongst us destroyers.'

'How bad?' Wally asked.

'*Montrose* and *Mackay* collided and grounded in the mêlée, I'm afraid. *Grenade*'s been sunk; *Jaguar, Greyhound, Intrepid* and poor old *Saladin* have all been hit. Ruddy awful…'

'How d'you know all this?'

'We have all the signals here as flotilla leader. The Stukas are having a field day in these restricted waters. *Lorina, Normannia* and *Fenella,* personnel ships, have been sunk, and *Canterbury* damaged. A "Clan" boat has bought it and several other merchants have been damaged. We're taking off many more troops now that the embarkation arrangements ashore are becoming organised.'

'How many troops have we brought off today?' Wally asked.

'About six hundred so far, but this ferrying out from the beaches is much too slow. This is our last daylight trip; the next one will be tonight, straight alongside the jetty in Dunkirk harbour.'

From 29th May onwards, all destroyers made the round trip during darkness. Route Z, the shortest, but now under enemy guns, could therefore be used more safely; however, for the captains and navigating officers of the ships, life was much more difficult.

On the trip to Dover, Wally managed to track down those few soldiers he had brought off in the whaler. He was worried about the woman, but he found her being cared for in the ward room. She had in fact just woken from a long sleep and, with *Malcolm*'s Sub-Lieutenant, was relishing a cup of strong tea. She looked up when Wally entered, her sad face surrounded by short black curls.

*'Merci, monsieur,'* she said: *'C'était charmant de vous...'* She hesitated, her black eyes welling with tears, before continuing in broken English. 'Eet was very good of you...' she continued slowly, but she couldn't go on as she remembered the horrible fate of her dead comrade. 'Georges was my fiancé,' she said. 'We had come all the way together from Béthune. He wanted to continue the fight from England...'

As she sat on the settee a wave of pity swept over Wally. This girl had courage.

'When we reach Dover,' he said, 'I'll take care of you.'

She momentarily enfolded his hand in both of hers as tears streamed down her face. Wally shyly proffered his grubby handkerchief.

*Malcolm* reached Dover at dusk, where she was immediately taken in hand by the excellent port organisation. A rapid re-ammunitioning and refuelling; a snatch of sleep while the troops were disembarked into the warehouses on the quays, where they were quickly put through the dispersal routine: into the waiting trains where, on the platforms, the women of

Dover took care of their men — tea, blankets and cigarettes all playing their part.

Wally went ashore with the French girl-soldier. For a moment they stood on one side while the stream of humanity slipped past them. She peered up at him in the darkness; she had a delicate face, a pale petal springing from the blue French officer's shirt which, though enormous for her neatness, she had, with Gallic chic, contrived to make attractive. Her slim figure allowed her to wear the French officer's trousers inconspicuously.

'When shall I see you again?' Wally asked. 'You'll be on your own, and I'd like to help you if you'd allow me.'

She smiled, shrugged with that expressive gesture of the French and shook her head. Wally extracted his propelling pencil and scribbled down his home address on a scrap of paper.

'That's my home. Where my mother lives. If you need help in this tight little island, just get in touch.'

She was carefully pronouncing the address: 'Greenvale,' she was saying slowly, 'Guildford Road — Farncombe — Surrey. Where is that, please?'

'South of London. You will get in touch?'

'Yes.'

'What's your name?' Wally asked shyly.

'Suzanne.' She squeezed his arm and turned away.

He handed her over to the WVS women and the French girl was gone, swallowed amongst the hordes of exhausted soldiers mustering on the platform. He slowly threaded his way back against the tide of men who, with only their rifles in their hands, had been plucked from the beaches: 13,752 from the beaches that day, 33,558 from Dunkirk harbour, including 2,000 wounded.

'Sea Dutymen close up?

Hardly had Wally laid his head on *Malcolm*'s ward-room settee than the routine pipe jerked him from his sleep of exhaustion. As he scrambled into the ward-room flat he bumped into David Mellis who, wiping his bleary eyes, was fumbling his way up the ladder.

'Better join up with me, Sub. Care to give me a hand?'

Wally helped David Mellis during the next few unforgettable days and nights. On the night of 30th May, *Malcolm* crumpled her bow on the piles of the jetty at Dunkirk. Tom Halsey drove his ship hard, his only concern being the evacuation of the troops. On the Friday night he made two round trips, embarking some 1,500 troops on each lift.

On the second trip back to Dunkirk in the early hours, fog came down. To add to the difficulties, *Malcolm*'s crumpled bow acted as a brake, so David had no accurate speed measurement. Though *Malcolm*'s bow wave was spectacular, the navigation was certainly difficult. *Malcolm* missed the buoy off Calais, which, in the low visibility and the clouds of black smoke from the pall which hung over Dunkirk, it was essential to find. David used the echo-sounder: four fathoms was soon showing. He manned the chains and, with the leadsman calling the soundings, *Malcolm* slowly backed out of the deep into which she had wrongly entered: the shallows prevented her from turning at rest and there was no room to manoeuvre.

*Malcolm* made nine trips in all, thus sharing the honours with *Sabre* for the number of cross-channel evacuations. It was during the last few nights that men were stretched to their limits, when, through lack of sleep, their nerves were at breaking point. *Malcolm* went alongside the jetty once more, three-deep against two other destroyers. The jetty seemed deserted. Wally, on the quarterdeck, cursed silently. Why couldn't the pongos organise themselves? He tried to pull himself together, realising suddenly that he was very tired — he had slept for only two hours during the last three days.

Then, to his amazement, the whole jetty seemed to move. He rubbed his eyes: he must be giddy with fatigue. There was a shouted order in the darkness and the thud of soldiers' heels stamping in unison. The crash of rifle butts and then the orderly movement of British soldiers marching on board in complete silence. A lump came into Wally's throat. These were the Guards, magnificent in their discipline.

It was at Calais — unlike Boulogne, where the rearguard had been withdrawn too early — that the Army were ordered to hold until the last man. This terrible sacrifice delayed the Germans from sweeping up the coast to overrun Dunkirk and the beaches. It was the steadfast sacrifice of the Guards, the Royal Tank and the rifle regiments at Calais that made the miracle of Dunkirk possible.

It was on *Malcolm*'s seventh trip that dawn broke before she was clear of the jetties. The last ship to load, she was on the inside of three destroyers berthed alongside. Wally was manning the 3-inch and adding to the barrage of gunfire being hurled at the diving Stukas. Dense black smoke was swirling through the harbour; flames and bomb bursts smothered the waterfront. Then, in the midst of this bedlam, whilst the finest troops from the rearguard column mustered on the jetties to await embarkation, there came a sudden lull.

In this strange stillness the plaintive skirl of bagpipes sadly drifted across the harbour. The strains of 'Over the Sea to Skye' floated across the water in the stillness of the new dawn. A great cheer rose from the ranks of the waiting soldiers on the jetties. Then Wally realised whence came this inspiring sound.

On *Malcolm*'s fo'c's'le, the figure of David Mellis, bagpipes crooked over his arm, stood alone in the eyes of the ship. There he stood, with bombs raining downwards, flame and smoke swirling through the harbour, playing the traditional tunes of his homeland.

This action was an inspiration to those who had waited for so long on the jetties. Asked later why he produced his bagpipes, David merely replied, 'The troops had nothing to do either, but to wait. I thought a counter-irritant might cancel out the other noises.'

The worst moment came for Wally in Dover, during the forenoon of June the third. The notice pinned outside David Mellis's cabin was still visible, though by now somewhat grubby: *Could you take your boots off? I live here.*

And underneath, for the benefit of the French soldier: *Ne mettez pas les bottines sur les drapeaux — j'habite ici.*

Wally had just stretched himself out for his first good sleep in days — they had made their last Dunkirk trip — when the bo'sun's mate's call shrilled from above:

'Cle-a-r lower deck. Muster on the iron deck.'

At 1130, Captain Halsey, who had just returned from the Headquarters in the Dover cliffs, stood on the torpedo tubes to address his men. His tired grey eyes swept slowly across them all.

'We've done our best. Altogether the ships have taken off three hundred thousand of our soldiers, the bulk of the Army. I thought we had carried out our last trip. I've just seen Admiral Ramsay — he tells me that the French, who are the last of the rearguard and who have been holding the line for us, have asked to be taken off tonight.' Tom Halsey paused, then looked at his men. 'I told the Admiral I'd ask you whether you'd make one more trip to bring off the French. We can't let them down, can we?'

A murmur rumbled from the 300 sailors grouped around their Captain. Then he jumped down from the tubes.

Wally's stomach sank. After letting go and relaxing, the moral effort to screw up one's courage again was almost an insuperable task. For over a week they had been at it, a long nightmare of horror and strain; the cheerfulness, the courage and inventiveness of the British soldier had left an indelible impression on his mind. As the German pincers closed and as the British rearguard fell back, the defence of Calais had become vital. The defenders had held until they could hold out no longer.

The last night of evacuation lay ahead. The Dutch were overrun, their royal family under Queen Wilhelmina having been transported to England on the *Hereward*. The Belgians had surrendered, and only just in time had the B.E.F. sealed off the advance of the Panzers along the northern shore. The French armies had been cut off from their British allies. No more R.A.F. squadrons could be spared over the beaches where the Luftwaffe had virtually undisputed control. Air Marshal Dowding dared risk no more fighter squadrons: he *had* to maintain an adequate defence fighter force for when the Luftwaffe made their onslaught upon the British Isles.

Tonight, the third of June, would be the last night, Wally knew: the Germans would be through to the beaches the next day. The French rearguard had been magnificent, by all accounts.

*Malcolm*'s ward room changed for dinner that night. In mess undress and bow ties they set off for France. 'I think we're shooting a bit of a line,' David said. 'Let's go in monkey jackets instead.'

'And bow ties,' the Sub said.

So, steaming into Dunkirk harbour at full speed, *Malcolm* took off her last load of French troops in the early hours. It was dawn when she finally reached mid-Channel on her return journey, the pall of smoke above Dunkirk the last memory of the horror to be etched into Wally's mind. *Malcolm* passed hundreds of small ships: drifters, Dutch *schuyts* commanded by R.N. Sub-Lieutenants, tugs, yachts, all staggering home with their last loads.

When ten miles east of Dover, *Malcolm* took in tow a broken-down French motor torpedo boat which had lost her propellers. The French Naval Commander-in-Chief, Vice-Admiral Abrial, Commandant du Nord, was on board, having been taken off at the last minute. He was transferred to *Malcolm*, who unfortunately — diverted by this interlude — forgot to hoist Tom Halsey's signal on entering harbour. Tom, an Old Etonian, had intended to enter harbour flying *Floreat Etona,* this day being the fourth of June.

On the quay Wally bumped into an R.N.V.R. Lieutenant, Robert Nye. Together they walked up to the castle to collect their orders. Nye was Captain of a Motor Anti-Submarine Boat, MASB 10; he had been operating off Calais and with his flotilla had taken part in the evacuation of Boulogne. Next it would be Le Havre and Cherbourg.

'At least it isn't all gloom,' Robert Nye said. 'Gort's back.' General Gort was the Commander-in-Chief of the British Expeditionary Force. 'Winnie had to send a personal envoy across to *order* him to return to England. Being Gort, he wouldn't leave his troops.'

Wally nodded and was silent.

'What was *Malcolm*'s worst moment?' Robert Nye asked.

Without hesitation, Wally replied: 'When we had to leave *Clan Macalister* off the beaches. She caught fire after bombing. Our navigating officer, David Mellis, tried to put out the fire by stuffing a hose down the after-hatch. The Captain, Tom Halsey, quite rightly decided he couldn't wait, because *Malcolm* was loaded full of troops and he had to get them back to Dover. The Master of *Clan Macalister* had asked for an escort, which Tom had to refuse because of the difference in speed. So the Master decided to linger about off the beaches to wait for a slower escort.'

'Asking for trouble, wasn't it?' Nye asked.

'She was bombed to hell. The casualties were frightful.'

The two men reached the castle offices in the cliff, where they reported to the enquiries desk. Ahead of them in the queue was another Sub-Lieutenant, a dark-haired man of average height with a pale, oval face, surrounded by a ginger beard.

'You've got a long wait ahead of you,' he said. 'I've been here over an hour.'

Robert Nye, being the oldest and the most senior, made the introductions. The bearded Sub introduced himself as Peter Dickens. He'd been the Sub of one of the tribal-class destroyers, *Somali*, who'd been involved in the abortive Norwegian campaign. He'd been yanked out of her and sent, like Wally, down to Dover.

'I was appointed mate of a Dutch *schuyt*,' Dickens said. 'The Dutch were marvellous and appeared not to resent me at all. Perhaps it was because they'd only just reached England after escaping from Holland.

'Anyway, I was told by the S.O.O. people to go to Dunkirk. "Why?" I asked. "You'll find out when you get there," I was told. For the past eight days I've been finding out!'

Robert Nye chuckled: Dickens was obviously a character.

Dickens was summoned into the office. 'So long,' he said, grinning. 'See you some day.'

Robert Nye went in next to make his report. Wally, on his own now, sat down and watched the exhausted faces as the men streamed in and out from this heart of Operation Dynamo. He asked the Wren officer at the desk what the final score was.

'Over 338,000,' she said. 'But at quite a price.'

Wally lifted his eyebrows.

'Over 230 ships lost,' she said, '28 being destroyers sunk or damaged.'

Wally was silent, the magnitude of the disaster suddenly sweeping over him. Britain and the Commonwealth were alone now, utterly alone. Their armies were intact but weaponless. The enemy was nineteen miles away, at Cap Gris Nez. In between, flowed the Channel — or the Ditch, as some called it.

*Our Last Ditch*, he thought. He'd ask for a small ship in the Channel. This was where he belonged now. This was where he'd fight. This cruelly impartial strip of water was where he'd live or die.

Robert Nye emerged, his face serious. 'You're next,' he said.

Walter Bruce straightened himself and pushed his way into the office.

# CHAPTER 3

*Stand to your Moat!*
*Autumn 1940 — Summer 1941*

*'Never give in, never give in, never, never, never … Never yield to force;*
*never yield to the apparently overwhelming might of the enemy.'*
Winston Churchill

It was August 1940 before Wally Bruce took his first command, Motor Launch 115, to sea with the Second M.L. Flotilla. He had spent six weeks working up his little vessel, six long weeks during which period the nation braced itself to resist the invader who was gathering his forces in the French Channel ports. The French nation had collapsed, and though many Frenchmen had braved all and escaped to England to continue the fight under General de Gaulle, Britain now stood alone. The world watched and waited for the destruction of this proud island.

Winston Churchill's clarion calls to the nation proclaimed Britain's defiance: the tragedies of Dakar and Oran proved to the world that this island was determined to honour its resolve, whatever disasters might befall it. The distasteful duty of eliminating the French fleet in these North African ports had been carried out by the Royal Navy to prevent the French warships falling into the hands of the Nazis.

Roosevelt, President of the United States, was now convinced of Britain's resolution: he immediately provided aid in the shape of armaments, the loan of fifty old destroyers, and the adoption of American responsibility for the protection of the North American continent by the lease of British bases in the West Indies.

The Italians, misled by their dictator, Mussolini, were dragged into the war at Hitler's behest. The free world held its breath as the Nazi invasion forces gathered, poised to strike across the Channel. The German Navy would not sail until the Luftwaffe had gained control of the skies above their invasion fleets. While the enemy waited for the Royal Air Force to be shot out of the skies, the British threw up bristling lines of defences along the coasts of England.

September slipped into October before the nation realised that it had not been overwhelmed by the Luftwaffe. It was recognised also that, because the gallant 'few' of the R.A.F. had won what Winston was calling the Battle of Britain, the Germans were not now dominating the English Channel. The ships of the Royal Navy could still operate in the Narrow Seas, though only by night when without fighter escort.

By mid-October, the rumours of the imminence of the German invasion decreased. On 13th September, following reports of invasion fleets and barge concentrations in all the Low Country and French ports, Boulogne was bombarded by *Royal Sovereign,* and Cherbourg by British destroyers. British anti-invasion patrols inshore, in mid-Channel and up the east coast, now numbered over one thousand vessels, from destroyers to trawlers.

To achieve these numbers, ships from the north-west approaches, from Plymouth and from the north-east, were taken off convoy duties and sent to the main threat: in the Channel and off the south-east coast. With no adequate protection the convoys were now virtually undefended, and the losses of merchant ships grew to terrible proportions. 'We can't go on like this,' the Prime Minister growled.

During the first weeks of October, the island's defences were hastily completed. Tank traps, barbed wire, pillboxes; the training of the Home Guard, the reorganisation of the British Army, the build-up of the Canadian divisions; the loan by America of fifty old destroyers — all these factors gradually began to have their psychological effects. Then, after rumours that tens of thousands of German invasion troops had been roasted in a sea of fire (Wally had seen one German corpse floating in the Channel), Britain began to breathe again. October surrendered to November. Gales lashed the coasts, the nights lengthened... no invasion force, not even German, could cross the Channel in these appalling conditions. Britain was safe from invasion by sea until the spring.

The Luftwaffe had changed its tactics after 15th September. Attacking now by night, Goering hurled thousands of bombers against British cities. They came in waves, the first low with incendiaries; the subsequent with high explosive from all heights to transform the winter nights into flaming hells. The rage of the Nazis upset Goering's strategy because, by the slaughtering of British civilians, Britain's resolve was strengthened. From these days also, under the direct leadership of Winston Churchill, all arms of the Services were imbued with the one guiding principle: to strike back at the enemy, to hit him as hard and as often as possible down the whole length of the Channel coast; to keep the enemy guessing and to extend him to the uttermost along the coasts of his enslaved Europe.

For the coastal forces the struggle was long, cold and bitter during the winter of 1940/41. With the small ships of both sides battling every night for control of the Narrow Seas, there was no mercy shown. British coastal convoys ran regularly twice a week from the Thames, both northwards and south-westwards. It was for this last duty that the motor launches were built. Constructed of marine plywood, these small craft were beginning to roll off the assembly lines; built in sections by Fairmiles all over the country, the various components were finally assembled in yards around the coast. The result was the 'A' class Fairmile, a sturdy launch, with excellent sea-keeping qualities; then came the 'B's and the future generations.

Wally, with his First Lieutenant, Sub-Lieutenant Christopher Jannaway, R.N.V.R., did not take long to become accustomed to their new ship, M.L. 115. Of sixty-five tons displacement and 112 feet long, she drew only five feet, fully loaded. Her high free-board made her relatively dry at sea, but with her clean lines and her twin Hall Scott petrol engines developing 1,200 brake horsepower, she could attain 18 knots at full power. She was fitted with an Asdic (anti-submarine detector) dome and carried ten depth charges, in addition to her armament of one 3-pounder, two strip Lewis and two Vickers machine guns which, much later, were to be replaced by an Oerlikon on a mounting aft. The flotilla was operated by Captain 'Reggie' Darke, the Commanding Officer of the Submarine Headquarters Base at H.M.S. *Dolphin*, Haslar Creek at Gosport.

One evening in December, Wally called on his Senior Officer, Lieutenant Peter Loasby, R.N., in 113, to collect information for the correction of the confidential books. Loasby was tall, dark-haired, with a weather-beaten face. He was respected by his C.O.s because he was efficient and a 'goer'. There were nine boats in the flotilla, all commanded by R.N.V.R. C.O.s, except for Monkton, the Divisional Commander, who was R.N.R.

Wally Bruce had just squared himself off for the evening meal when there was a tap on the ward room lintel. The bo'sun's mate, cap in hand, was sheepishly peering round the corner of the bulkhead.

'There's a Wren here, sir, with a personal message from Captain Darke.'

'Show her in, please.'

The slight figure in dark-blue serge was shown into the ward room, which she nervously entered. Her Wren's cap, jauntily askew over one ear, revealed her dark hair, and from beneath the broad forehead gleamed two piercingly black eyes. Her small mouth twitched with amusement as she held out the sealed envelope.

Wally stood, speechless. 'Well, I…'

'I thought it must be you,' Suzanne said. 'I saw your name in the S.D.O. and wondered.' She looked up shyly. 'I'm glad.'

There was still the unmistakable French accent, still the trace of steel about her which the Dunkirk tragedy had implanted. Even in her Wren's uniform, she was impeccably chic.

'I've changed my name,' she said. 'I'm Suzanne Noyce now.'

'Why'd you do that?'

'All we Free French take different names. The Gestapo can't trace our relatives. At least we can spare them the torture.'

Wally nodded. 'Suzanne Noyce,' he repeated quietly. 'That's a very pleasant name.'

Her black eyes met his, held them for a moment, then turned away shyly. 'You haven't asked me why I'm here. I've got a message for you. Very important.' Half turning towards him so that the tip of her diminutive nose tilted upwards, she produced the message and watched the query reflected in Wally's face.

'Yes,' she said. 'Captain Darke.' She held out the pad for him to read, and by accident his hand closed on hers. As he read the message his fingers tightened. He felt the response, a mutual signal stirring between them.

'Are you the naughty ship?' she asked, the banter now gone. 'He's very angry.'

Apparently two culprits, presumably from the Second M.L. Flotilla, had 'borrowed' two of the chickens from the brood of hens of which Captain Darke was very fond; a trail of blood had led down to the M.L. pontoons. Wally chuckled. Only Shaw-Brundell's boys would have the neck — if that was not an unfortunate metaphor!

'It's not funny,' Suzanne said. 'The Captain has called in the — how d'you call 'em — the C.I.D.?' She looked at him, the corners of her mouth puckered in amusement, her lips pursed. Wally felt his heart stir as he looked down at her; such a tiny, neat person...

'I'll ask my men,' he said. 'I'm sure they wouldn't have pinched the Captain's chickens. But you know what they'll say, don't you, Sukie?'

She shook her head, her hand still held by his.

'"Wot, *me*, sir? Not *me*, sir..." That's what they'll all say.' He paused as he saw that she was not responding. A cloud was passing over her face as terrible memories flooded back. 'Seeing you again has brought back Dunkirk.'

She hesitated. 'Thank you, Wally. It was —'

'Don't talk about it,' Wally interrupted, gently removing his hand. He placed his forefinger across her cheek to catch the tears welling in her eyes. 'You're not alone, you know...'

She tried to smile, but her words were barely audible. 'It helps to talk about it, my friend,' she whispered. 'Now I must finish my duties. I have other ships to visit with the message.'

'Sukie...'

'Yes?'

'Will you come out with me tonight? We can talk then.'

Her hand closed on his forearm as she turned away from him. Her head was half tilted up at him, her oval face vibrant with mixed emotions. With her other hand she patted an errant black curl back into place beneath her Wren's cap. She nodded, unable to speak.

'Outside the main gate. Before the blitz starts... about seven-thirty.'

She turned quickly and hurried from him towards the short ladder leading up to the bridge. He turned to collect his cap so that he could see her off the gangway, but when he reached the upper deck she had gone. He could see her trim blue figure tripping along the jetty. She did not look back.

Later that evening Loasby sent for his commanding officers. 'Someone,' he said, 'and it *must* be the Second... has stolen two of Captain Darke's chickens.' He paused, looking slowly round his C.O.s. All were stony-faced, particularly Shaw-Brundell. 'Reggie Darke is livid, and the whole of *Dolphin* is shaking in its shoes while this emergency is on. The C.I.D. has been called in. They have traced the trail of chicken blood to our pontoon.'

Shaw-Brundell was a dark-haired and gay rogue, notorious for his escapades; his was a wild crew and, so the 'buzz' went, two of his 'skates' had effected this cutting-out expedition with considerable verve.

It was not until Loasby took his flotilla into mid-Channel that the matter was again mentioned, when, as Senior Officer, he received a signal from Shaw-Brundell's boat on the outer wing of the convoy: *To S.O., M.L. 113. Excellent chicken for luncheon today.* During the C.I.D.'s search for the corpses, the two skates had hidden the evidence in the 3-pounder's Ready-Use locker.

Wally would never forget his first convoys. The winter of 1940 was bitterly cold. The wind cut straight through him and he was always wet, his body craving sleep. The Channel East and Channel West convoys continued twice a week. The fear of the magnetic and acoustic mine affected everyone's mind: never did this terror entirely vanish, particularly for those dedicated men toiling in the bowels of the engine rooms below the waterline. Because of the noise from the M.L.'s propellers and engines, the balloon ships towed the launches from Ramsgate up to Southend. Later, because of the long tow round from South Foreland, the M.L.s broke off at Ramsgate, where they were locked into the inner harbour.

One easterly, and one westerly convoy per week, or three convoys every ten days, was the normal routine. From the moment of leaving the convoy was escorted by one or two Hunt-class destroyers, one of whom carried the Senior Officer of the escort, who usually led in the van; and by a flotilla of M.L.s who operated in pairs, six on the seaward side and two on the inshore flank of the convoy, which was in two lines ahead, its columns disposed abeam. A Submarine Chaser or an M.L. usually brought up the rear as 'tail-end Charlie' while one or two more acted as a physical screen on the seaward beam. The convoys formed up at Southend, ran to Portsmouth, then on to Dartmouth and finally to Plymouth. The procedure was reversed twice weekly. If possible, the C.E. convoy's E.T.A. in the Straits of Dover was early dawn, so that the ships could be in the shelling area between Ramsgate and Folkestone during darkness, but approaching the Goodwins — the Graveyard, as it was called — at first light: the convoy would then be able to avoid the masts and funnels of the wrecks sunk in the middle of the Channel.

Wally spent Christmas Day 1940 escorting a coal ship of the Southern Electricity Company from Portsmouth to Shoreham; she was rust-splotched, with a distinctive white line painted around her gunwales. Wally told the collier to precede him through the Looe channel, off Selsey Bill. The tidal stream ran strongly through these narrows, and Wally allowed the collier ample room ahead of him. The cloud base was low, but there was considerable glare from the hidden sun.

'These Shoreham runs are becoming monotonous, Number One. Thank goodness we're going up with C.E. 22 off The Owers after delivering this old tub to Shoreham.'

'Is that the form, sir? Good. I could do with another evening in Ramsgate.'

'At The Rising Sun, of course?'

'How *did* you guess, sir?'

Both men chuckled. An evening at the inn was their relaxation, once they were safely 'locked in' at Ramsgate. Once inside the lock gates no one could call them out for at least twelve hours. The Rising Sun, still standing there defiantly amid the ruins from the shelling, was a wonderful pub, extending a real warmth of hospitality to the men of the convoy escorts. Even the wash-places were popular: there was always a queue for the right-hand urinal, which had emblazoned on its glazed surface a portrait of Adolf Hitler. Mussolini's pug-like features, on the left-hand side of the other two conveniences, remained virtually unmolested.

Number One, whose lanky body was sprawled over the bridge rail, was peering idly over 115's stern. He spoke sharply but did not raise his voice: 'Don't look now, sir, but I think we're being followed.'

Wally slowly turned round. There, a mile inshore, were the silhouettes of two low-flying fighters. They were banking slowly and turning towards, barely fifty feet above the sea.

'Can't be…' Wally said.

'Yes, sir. I think so. Double bluff on the part of the Luftwaffe…' The small ships had been deceived before by this manoeuvre of the enemy's.

'Don't man your guns until the last moment,' Wally snapped. 'Warn the pom-pom, Number One, not to take any interest until the last moment.'

'Aye, aye, sir.' Jannaway picked up the telephone and spoke into its mouthpiece. Wally sauntered over to the port side of the bridge to lean nonchalantly over the bridge rail. From the corner of his eye he watched the two Messerschmitt 109s enlarging at every second.

'Thank goodness we were at Action Stations, Number One. Everybody ready?'

'Yes, sir — standing by.'

Wally could feel the tension tightening throughout the ship. He'd been caught napping once before, but not this time. He could see the gun's crew slouching upon the mounting of their new pom-pom, where they were lighting up their cigarettes. The yellow snouts of the 109s were visible now — only five hundred yards away — and now, suddenly opening up their throttles, they zoomed in on the M.L.'s port quarter.

'Open fire!' Wally yelled. Number One dropped his hand. Every gun in the little ship opened up, to the splendid accompaniment of the single 'Chicago piano', the pom-pom.

The two Messerschmitts were in line ahead, with the rear fighter stupidly in the slipstream of its leader. As they dived into the hail of fire, the leader sheered off to fly parallel to the M.L. at only two hundred yards' range.

The pom-pom's crew were so astounded that they could barely train their mounting fast enough. Wally watched the single barrel of the pom-pom pumping away, its bell-shaped flame-guard pointing directly at its target, the leading Messerschmitt.

The rear fighter jerked suddenly; black smoke gobbed from its engine, then engulfed the machine, until it dived into the sea off The Owers. There was a yell of exultation as the white plume of water leapt from the sea where the fighter splashed.

'That makes it fifteen-love, I think,' Wally said. 'Follow the collier, Number One.'

They watched the unharmed Messerschmitt swoop high into the clouds where it vanished in a flip of fury, bound southwards whence it had come.

'Not good shooting, Number One, but effective.'

Jannaway's gaunt features broke into a grin: this was high praise from his Scottish captain. 'Shall I fall out Action Stations, sir?'

'No, not until we deliver the goods. But you can splice mainbrace at their quarters.'

Thus M.L. 115's first kill was celebrated on Christmas Day, 1940. At 1330, she anchored off Shoreham entrance, while the collier proceeded into harbour between the piers which stretched, like twin fingers, into the Channel. The launch wallowed at her anchor, whilst her company, except for the lookout on the bridge, ate their Christmas dinner, a somewhat unusual ceremony, ably assisted by an extra tot of rum. However, sobriety was the order of the day, because, after an afternoon's sleep, M.L. 115 weighed at 1515 to join the convoy CE 22 which was plodding up from The Owers.

'Sweepers on the starboard bow, sir,' the starboard lookout reported. 'Range three miles.'

The first indications of an approaching convoy, these minesweeping trawlers cleared the swept channel, performing their monotonous and hazardous duty daily. Their squat hulls with their high, flared bows, their tall funnels streaming black smoke to leeward, moved swiftly east towards Beachy Head. Then, as dusk enveloped them, the darkened shapes of the convoy slipped, one by one, into sight. Wally identified himself with the leading 'Type One' Hunt, *Cattistock*. By 1640, it was dark and M.L. 115 had taken up her station as tail-end Charlie on the port wing and on the inshore flank of the convoy screen.

Beachy Head loomed up, a huge mass, frightening with its immensity in the darkness. A ribbon of whiteness stretched indefinitely on the M.L.'s port beam, where the seas crashed at the foot of Beachy. Wally resisted the urge to ease over to starboard, not only because his duty was to follow the dim blue stern light of the M.L. ahead of him, but because the after ship in the convoy's front column was less than fifty yards distant. Her stern bucked and wallowed in the long swell which was building up astern as the wind freshened from the south west.

Wally drew his duffle closer around him and tugged at the Balaclava enveloping his ears, upon which his cap rested. The cold was excruciating tonight: there must be many degrees of frost, for even the wet wooden grating on which he was standing, usually slippery and greasy, was white with frost, as were the edges of the plating of the bridge side, to which his gloves stuck. He once again raised his binoculars to his eyes to follow the blue stern light of M.L. 117, who was well to port of the convoy. Suddenly a shimmering ribbon of whiteness appeared ahead and 117 seemed to swing rapidly to port. Wally went hard-a-starboard to avoid his next ahead.

Lieutenant Duff-Still, R.N.V.R., was Commanding Officer of 117. He too at the last minute had seen this thin white line in the darkness: the usual confused seas of wind against tide off Dungeness, he had thought, and pressed on.

Less than half a minute later there was an unpleasant crunch; his M.L. shuddered beneath him and Duff-Still was forced to conclude that he had grounded hard on Dungeness Spit.

'Good God!' he blurted. 'That's a line of snow!' He turned to his First Lieutenant, who had come up to relieve him. 'What does A do now?'

There was an unpleasant silence.

'Asdic doesn't work, sir,' came an indignant report from the A/S voicepipe.

'I know, you idiot; we're aground.'

'And on a falling tide, sir,' Number One added ungraciously.

117 settled like a duchess into a relatively upright posture.

'Well, I'd better report our position,' Duff-Still said. 'Dig out the Asdic dome, First Lieutenant.'

'Aye, aye, sir.'

The Captain shinned down the anchor cable while his bewildered hands set about retrieving the Asdic dome. He gingerly walked across what must have been one of the most heavily mined beaches on the south coast. Dungeness lighthouse rose huge, gaunt and ghostly white into the night sky. Duff-Still strode up to the door of the keeper's house.

'Excuse me,' he said to the surprised face at the door. 'I've arrived. May I please telephone Dover Operations?'

The next morning a tug appeared from Dover and towed 117 off at high water. Duff-Still shamefacedly rejoined his flotilla at Chatham two days later.

The Second M.L. Flotilla continued with its convoy work throughout the long and bitterly cold winter of 1940/41. When in harbour they were bombed at night; when at sea they were savaged by day in the Dover Strait by Stukas and 109s. Sleep was all that mattered to those serving in the small ships; blessed oblivion which, for a moment, blotted out the fears that gnawed like a maggot inside a man's mind. Then, miraculously, spring was upon them and the seventeen-hour nights became rapidly shorter. June came with its fogs and its long spells of calm, its long days and short nights. Though the threat of invasion had receded, the Battle of the Narrow Seas continued relentlessly.

# CHAPTER 4

### *A Cruel Night*

Wally had been in M.L.s nearly nine months and he had grown to know Loasby well. Peter was a grand Senior Officer: fair, decisive and fun. With his rugged, weather-beaten face, Peter Loasby was the scourge of officialdom ashore: he castigated any 'pusser' who was slack in producing stores or armament for the Second M.L. Flotilla. Loasby's C.O.s and his troops respected him and produced their best.

At 1030 on 8th July 1941, the Second M.L. Flotilla was setting forth again from Chatham for the next C.W. to Portsmouth. It made its rendezvous with the convoy which was already weighing off Southend and setting course for the North Foreland. By 1750 it was off the Goodwins, where thick fog suddenly engulfed the straggling mass of ships. On orders from the Senior Officer in the Hunt destroyer, *Atherstone,* the convoy anchored hurriedly where it was.

Wally, in 115, was now at the rear of the seaward screen, Peter Loasby being up ahead. On the radio telephone Wally could listen to *Atherstone* talking to the escorts. The convoy was to remain where it was until the fog lifted, firstly because the Channel seemed to be crammed with thousands of floating pit props from a sunken ship; and secondly because something strange seemed to be occurring a few hundred yards away on the far side of the shifting sands of the Goodwins.

'Listen, Number One, what's that?'

Above the sound of the tidal stream swirling against their cable came the unmistakable rattling of small anchor chains.

There was a pause, then the guttural shouting of commands in German; then more rattlings from anchor cables.

Number One turned, a grin on his freckled face. 'E-boats, I think, sir. Having as much trouble with the fog as we are.'

So, for three hours, an E-boat flotilla was anchored on the seaward side of the Goodwins, whilst the straggled convoy waited tensely less than a quarter of a mile away across the sands.

'At least the Hun doesn't know these waters as well as we do,' Wally muttered. 'It'll be a matter of who can weigh first.'

Then, at 2330, the fog began to lift. *Weigh,* ordered *Atherstone.*

Wally listened to the ships surrounding him, still invisible in the fog, their cables clanking home. Then, in the eerie stillness, the outline of the colliers and the tramps slipped past on the tide.

'Weigh,' Wally ordered, 'and keep your eyes skinned for E-boats.'

'Anchors aweigh, sir,' came the cry from the fo'c's'le.

'Half ahead together.'

In the darkness, M.L. 115 sounded her way along the edge of the channel which skirted the Goodwin Sands. The lightship, so often machine-gunned by the Luftwaffe, was no longer there to help. Wally's eyes ached as he peered into the swirling wisps of fog.

'Keep your eyes skinned, lookouts.'

The danger of being run down by the convoy was worse than the hazard from the E-boats, which were now lurking to pounce.

'Right ahead, sir,' Number One shouted. 'Object in the water.'

Wally stared ahead until his eyes watered.

'*Where*, for God's sake?'

'There, sir…'

Then he saw it, a huge gantry and a mast, looming down upon them from out of the water: the mast from a sunken ship in the Graveyard.

'Hard-a-starboard.'

The M.L. responded immediately. Then, as she began to swing, a funnel reared from the water like a black finger.

'Hard-a-port. Full astern together.'

The M.L. shuddered to the power. Downtide and out of control, she lost her way; she stopped and — as Wally waited, gripping the bridge screen — she slid past the funnel. The gunners on the fo'c's'le had rushed over to bear off their boat from the collision as she slipped between the funnel and the sunken mast.

'Phew,' Wally whispered. 'A near one.'

Then they were out of the Graveyard and swinging down on the tide past South Foreland and on towards Dover.

Visibility by now had improved to half a mile. The ships, every man jack of them, were feeding their boilers all they could take. Black smoke streamed from their tall, ancient funnels.

'Their stokers are burning all they've got tonight, sir.'

'Socks and all, Number One. What a night! Not only E-boats, dammit, but now we're entering the shelling area.' South-west Folkestone buoy was flashing ahead, while the cliffs of Dover loomed to starboard.

'There they go…' Number One pointed towards France, where the horizon flickered suddenly with pinpoints of light.

'Stand by for shelling,' Wally ordered.

The young captain reached for his steel helmet, put it squarely on his head and tapped its crown for luck. Methodically he adjusted the strap so that it reached only the tip of his chin: he had once seen a man's neck broken by the shock of the helmet flying back against the blast when the strap had been fastened beneath the chin.

At the head of the convoy an orange flame leapt, and a sharp crack reverberated against the cliffs as the first shells exploded on the water. Spouts of foam cascaded upwards and golden plumes of spray showered gently down, lit by the explosions of the next salvos.

It was nearly two hours before the convoy was through the shelling area. The lookouts relaxed and started to sweep the horizon with their binoculars, their shadowy figures a blur in the wings of the bridge.

To the eastward the moon swung into the heavens, masked from the convoy by her gossamer veil of high cirrus. Night became as day, the pale luminosity spreading across the glassy sea, grey and mysterious with its undulations from the long swell.

'A grand night. I should raise Dungeness Light in an hour or so,' Wally mused. The lighthouses along the south coast would, upon request from the convoys, illuminate for twenty minutes while the ships passed down-Channel. Unfortunately this procedure was now a certain indication for any lurking enemy.

Wally watched the convoy ahead of him, its two lines well established, each ship within three cables of the next ahead. There were sixteen ships in all, so the leaders stretched invisibly ahead, lost in the pale moonlight, where the milky streak of the horizon merged into the sky. Up there *Atherstone*, as Senior Officer of the escort, she was responsible for the safe arrival of the convoy. She must be feeling relieved, thought Wally: a run-of-the-mill C.W. so far.

He fumbled for his pouch and lit his pipe in the safety of the chart table, because in tonight's moonlight there was no fear of discovery from the lighted match: the ships stood up like houses upon this silvery sea. Wally smiled to himself as he puffed contentedly at the tobacco.

Suzanne disliked his smoking. They had spent the evening together three nights ago. She had waited for him outside *Dolphin*'s main gate, hidden in the shadows under the elms opposite Haslar Hospital. His heart had beaten faster as he approached her, a trim little person in blue serge, the gas mask slung over her shoulder. He had saluted, and she had laughed as she looked upwards, her face a faint oval of light in the darkness.

'Officers don't salute ratings,' she said, placing the tips of her fingers on the single gold stripe on his arm, but Wally had not responded. Instead, he had walked her across the playing field alongside *Hornet* (the first M.T.B. base) while they decided what to do.

'I've got to be back by ten-thirty,' Suzanne had said. 'There's not much time.'

The Heinkels had droned overhead then, dropping their incendiaries upon Gosport and Portsmouth, which already were twinkling with pinpoints of fire. The raid decided the young man and woman: arm in arm they hurried across the footbridge of Haslar Creek and into the slums of Gosport town which were, by now, well ablaze. The couple picked their way between the maze of snake-like fire hoses until they reached a rope barrier stretching across the road.

'No further,' the tin-hatted air raid warden ordered. 'There's a landmine down there,' and he pointed to where two men were running, bent double, down the street. They were paying out rope and shouting at a family who had rushed out of a burning house. A woman with hair tumbling down her neck came staggering haltingly towards Wally and Suzanne, a dead child cradled in her arms. As she approached, Wally could see her crazed face, her mouth working soundlessly, two children tugging at her skirts as she stumbled down the road.

Suzanne dipped under the ropes to take the woman into her arms. Then, comforting her, the French girl brought her back from under the rope barricade.

'He's still in there... the mother sobbed uncontrollably. 'Little Billy's in there...' and her head jerked back towards the inferno from which she had escaped. Her lined face, wet with tears and streaked with dirt, gleamed in the glare of the flames. Her eyes were glazed and, with the dead child still cradled in her arms, she was the epitome of the world's suffering womanhood. She began crooning to the lifeless bundle and swaying rhythmically from side to side.

Wally ducked beneath the cordon. He never looked back as he ran, slithering and tripping over the hoses, past the warden who was shouting obscenely at him. The house was less than twenty yards away now, a semi-detached Victorian building with a bow window. Flames were beginning to lick around the porch and already the roof was ablaze, pinpoints of intense white flames leaping where the incendiaries had lodged.

The heat was almost beyond bearing. Wally ripped off his reefer and wrapped it around his shoulders and head. He nipped up the two steps and thrust inwards through the open door, from which belched gouts of smoke and flame. Taking a deep breath, he put down his head and strode into the inferno.

It was not as hot inside as he had feared. He came up all-standing against the staircase, the banister of which was already alight; this gave him a lead through the swirling smoke and towards the stairway, up which he scrambled in answer to the screams of the small boy above. The landing was ablaze. As he leapt across it, he felt the staircase collapsing beneath him.

He found the boy in a back bedroom. Billy was paralysed by fear; his eyes wide circles of terror, he stood in the corner, a blanket held up before him to ward off the flames, which were already licking along the floor. The ceiling had collapsed, and the updraught of air was roaring through the roofless attic and into the sky.

Wally scooped up the boy in the crook of his arm. He slung the blanket around them both and stumbled, reeling and gasping, for the back window, which he kicked outwards.

'Go on, Billy. Shin down this...'

Wally watched the boy as he was lowered, fastened to the blanket, twelve feet below to the ground.

'*C'mon, mister...*' Billy waited there, with crashing timber and flying glass collapsing around him, until Wally had landed, a struggling heap beside him on the ground. Wally felt the boy's hand tugging him to his feet. Then, leading the way, Billy took his rescuer gingerly over the piles of smashed tiles and smouldering timber which had collapsed into the back yard. They scrambled into the street at the rear, where they saw a group of men pointing towards them, whistles shrilling at their lips. The men were waving and, even from this distance, Wally noticed the anxiety in their blackened faces. Picking up the boy, he put down his head and ran.

Wally smiled to himself in the moonlight on the bridge of his M.L. All was well with the world now: the ships were in station, the night was warm and calm, but what a wonderful night that had been with Suzanne... and the landmine had not exploded. He'd never forget the mother's rapture at being united with her Billy, a joy which had almost compensated for the death of her other child. Suzanne had mothered the pathetic little family — the father was away at sea in submarines — and had escorted them to the reception centre near the ferry in Gosport High Street.

'I've never really hated before,' Wally told her, as they walked back together, arm in arm towards the footbridge. 'It's not a pleasant feeling.'

Suzanne had pressed his arm. She said nothing for the moment; then, not looking up, she poured her heart out to him. At the bridge, Wally stopped and enfolded her in his arms. She nestled there, her body heaving convulsively with uncontrollable sobbing as she remembered her dead fiancé and his horrible death. Then she had pulled herself together and, standing close to him, had told him of her parents, who had been caught up with the stream of refugees. It was on the road that she had last seen them.

She stood there motionless, her arms slowly encircling his waist. There was peace in their hearts as they looked at one another, sharing the serenity of mutual understanding.

'Sukie,' Wally had whispered. 'Let me take care of you.'

Her arms tightened. She looked up at him, a sad smile on her pale face.

'Let me kiss you.'

She shook her head. She loosened her arms and pushed him gently from her.

'No,' she had whispered. 'Not yet, *mon chéri*...' She had tidied herself up, pushing back the curls under her cap, then she had looked him squarely in the face. 'Try to understand, Wally. It's too soon after François. He's still too near me. Perhaps, later...'

Wally knew then that, for the first time as a responsible man, he'd fallen really in love. That other girl he'd met in Edinburgh was nothing, nothing to this... and even here on his M.L.'s bridge, in the middle of the Channel, when he thought of

Suzanne a dull ache, a physical pain slowly suffused his body where his heart should have been.

'All ships *London-Vinegar; London-Vinegar,* Square Two…'

The loudspeaker crackled from the bridge screen. Wally lunged for the alarm-push. The rattlers sounded and men scrambled from below, duffles flapping and tin hats askew as they rushed to their Action Stations.

'Suspicious vessel in sight, Square Two, Number One,' Wally said, peering through his binoculars. Only the swish of the bow wave disturbed the silence of the night as M.L. 115 cut her way through the glassy surface.

'Vis. is poor to the southward,' the First Lieutenant said. 'Difficult to distinguish the horizon from the sea.'

Obscured by the high cirrus cloud, the moon traced silvery streaks towards the horizon where, mysteriously, they merged into the darkness. A blue light flickered from the M.L. on the seaward quarter. Pike, the signalman, grabbed his lamp to reply.

'From S.O.,' Pike repeated. '*Atherstone reports two suspicious vessels, Square Two.*'

Wally grew impatient. Nothing. The hands had missed enough sleep already. Ten minutes later the loudspeakers crackled again:

'From Atherstone*: Vessels identified.*'

Wally sighed. He was sick of false alarms and of having to turn out his weary men.

'Fall out, Action Stations.'

Once again the convoy settled down to its journey westwards, plumes of black smoke trailing from the jaunty funnels of the old tramps. The tide had now turned, and the convoy was making good only 4 knots. By one o'clock in the morning they were still batting westwards, with Dungeness

Light barely abeam. The flashing light sent its pencil ray sweeping across the horizon for the twenty minutes while the convoy was in the vicinity. This was long enough, however, to betray the ships to the lurking enemy.

*It's too bright for E-boats, anyway,* Wally thought. *The western horizon's clear now, as bright as day. Reckon I can have a pipe in this visibility.*

He turned to the lookouts. 'Carry on smoking.'

'Thank you, sir.'

Gnarled hands fumbled for hidden 'roll-me-owns' and eager lips dragged at dank tobacco which was lit from the smouldering slow-match hanging by the chart table. Wally puffed contentedly at his favourite pipe and settled down on the hinged wooden seat which was fixed to the bridge side. One arm over the 'splinter-mattresses' which festooned the bridge, he swept the horizon with his binoculars.

Nothing in sight. *Might be a peacetime manoeuvre,* he thought. *Royal Sovereign Lightship, Beachy Head next, and then we're nearly there.*

The convoy was an impressive sight. On either bow stretched two straight lines of merchant ships, the largest of which was only about 2,000 tons. To seaward of them, small dots of M.L.s chugged onwards, dipping and curvetting in the long swell. The invisible moon, screened by a film of fleecy cloud, cast her light upon a sea that ran like quicksilver.

Wally sighed contentedly. *Wish all convoys were like this,* he thought as he stretched his legs.

A prolonged roar rumbled from ahead, reverberating across the stillness. Wally's head jerked upwards as he jammed the binoculars to his eyes. A dull glow flickered from somewhere ahead. Then, as he peered, a shattering explosion from the head of the starboard column split the brooding silence.

Another roar followed in quick succession. In the port column a huge spout of water leapt upwards.

'Mines!' Wally gasped. They had run into their own minefield.

Men were already streaming from below to man their guns, but before Wally could press the night alarm buzzer, a shock hit the hull of the little M.L. as another ship blew up in the port column, only half a mile distant. A searing orange flame drenched the sky as Wally focused his glasses, but there was nothing to be seen; nothing but a frothing, heaving mass of water.

'My God!' he whispered. 'How horrible!'

There was nothing left, nothing.

'Stop both engines!' Wally shouted down the voicepipe.

The M.L. lost way and glided to a stop. Wally dashed to the chart table and ran his eye over the thin pencil line which represented his boat's course.

'We're in the swept channel,' he argued. '... strange!'

The truth hit him: *Atherstone* had been hoodwinked. The ships which she had challenged had, in fact, been enemy mine-laying destroyers. They had laid their 'eggs' ahead of the convoy, and had streaked, like assassins, back to France.

Urgently the loudspeaker crackled again.

'All ships, repeat all ships, act independently, and proceed via swept channel to Portsmouth. Enemy have laid mines. M.L. 115 recover survivors. Acknowledge.'

'Pretty obvious,' Wally muttered as he reached for the R/T transmitter. 'Message received,' he transmitted.

The remaining ships of the convoy were already growing smaller as the distance widened, black smoke now pouring from their funnels as the convoy desperately forged ahead to clear the danger area. Then he noticed that the last ship in the starboard column had started to haul out of line to port.

*She's trying to pick up survivors,* thought Wally. He moved to the voicepipe. 'Full ahead both!'

He felt the tremor of the launch as she gathered way, the pulse from her engines pounding in the engine room.

'This ought to trigger off any remaining mines,' Wally muttered. 'I'm sitting on top of a minefield and they may be acoustics.'

The M.L. closed the obstinate collier who was now two hundred yards on Wally's starboard beam. He picked up the microphone of the loud hailer.

'Get back into position, please. Get back into station,' he ordered.

'Get out of my blasted way. I'm picking up survivors!' a Geordie voice shouted back across the water. Wally hesitated as he once more picked up the microphone but, as he did so, an explosion rent the air. A searing heat sent him reeling against the compass. His head spun as the shock struck the sides of the M.L., so that she listed suddenly from the impact.

A curtain of red and green flames leapt skywards, roaring into the night. Wally staggered and clutched the bridge side, as into his consciousness was stencilled a scene he would never forget. The bows of the collier had disappeared and, where once they had been, a seething mass of debris and foam boiled and hissed. The ship's back was broken, her funnel leaning drunkenly for'd. Her stern was cocked out of the water, so that her propellers still threshed the air with slow beats, while the screams of dying men wailed through the night.

'Help me! For God's sake save us!' came a thin cry across the water from a man flailing helplessly.

'Hard-a-port, full ahead together! Steer for that man in the water, Cox'n.'

'Aye, aye, sir.'

'Might as well save him, Number One. This other ship's a goner!' Wally called. 'Stand by to pick him up, port side-to.' As the M.L. closed on the man struggling in the water, desperate cries from other drowning men drifted through the night from all sides.

'Stop both, stand by to recover!' But as the M.L. went full astern to halt alongside the dark head in the oily sea, the man disappeared with only a ripple to mark his watery grave.

Sickened, Wally turned away.

'Two men, starboard beam, sir,' the starboard lookout shouted, pointing with outstretched arm.

'Hard-a-starboard, slow ahead together!' and the M.L. slid alongside another group of struggling men.

'Catch this line and come alongside the scrambling net,' a voice shouted on the fo'c's'le. A heaving line snaked through the air to plop across the men, who grabbed it. Gently, slowly, they were pulled alongside, where strong hands snatched them from the hungry deeps.

'Look at that, sir!' the starboard lookout yelled. Wally's head jerked upwards.

The stern of the doomed ship was less than a hundred yards away, hanging poised between sky and water and looming some fifty feet into the air. She was settling fast, ready for her final plunge.

From the port quarter of her transom, a seaman hung head downwards, caught by his feet in the bight of a rope. He was swinging to and fro like a pendulum from the slow motion of the swell; frantically he snatched at the rope to heave himself upwards to reach the slanting deck. His body was jerking like a marionette on a string. A silence gripped the men as they watched the pitiful struggles of the doomed seaman, whose sobs floated across the diminishing space that separated the two ships wallowing in the water.

'I can't let this happen even if she takes us with her,' Wally whispered to himself as he sprang for the voicepipe. 'Slow ahead port, hard-a-starboard!'

The M.L. slid in under the counter of the towering transom. The dark mass hanging above the little ship's fo'c's'le blacked out the sky. Slowly, foot by foot, the M.L.'s bow edged nearer. Wally crouched low over the voicepipe to con her with every ounce of skill and concentration he possessed.

'Midships, slow astern together.'

So close were they, he could hear the gurgle of water as it lapped along the stern of the merchant ship, where he could plainly see the rusty rudder jammed to port. The black mass hung and plunged in the swell, fifteen, ten feet above the M.L.'s bows.

'She's going, sir!' yelled a voice from the fo'c's'le.

'Grab him, go on, grab him! Cut the rope!' Wally shouted. He could bear to look no longer, but waited for the rending crash as the ship plunged down upon them.

Frantic hands grappled for the dangling body. Stretching over the guard rails, they clutched and reached again.

'Knife! No! Cut, cut!' was all Wally could hear from his helpless position on the bridge. A blade gleamed on the fo'c's'le.

'Astern! Go astern, sir!' a man shouted from the fo'c's'le.

Wally glanced over the bridge. A crumpled figure sprawled across the guard rails.

'Full astern together!' Wally yelled down the voicepipe. His knuckles showed white in the pale moonlight. The engines coughed into life. The huge mass plunged and slid downwards, towards the M.L.'s fo'c's'le.

The little ship quivered as she gathered sternway; faster, faster she gathered way and glided astern. Metal screeched as it tore apart, but as suddenly the sickening sound ceased. The M.L. shook herself and leapt astern as she came free, like a cork from a bottle.

'Stop both!'

The M.L. lost way as her company watched the death throes of the collier. Already nothing but the counter remained. For a moment she hung there, her 'red duster' hanging limp in the still night. Then, with a rush, she went. The water boiled for an instant, debris shooting to the surface. Then she was gone.

The port lookout, a young seaman of eighteen, was vomiting over the side. It was all Wally could do not to keep him company, but mercifully more urgent problems demanded his immediate concentration.

Only the pathetic flotsam, which marked the final resting place of these brave ships, floated upon the silver ocean that stretched before them. Wally and his company were now alone, dependent upon themselves. They drifted upon the surface of a freshly sown minefield and there would be little hope for them if they touched off a mine now.

Wally checked his doubtful position in the chart.

'Slow ahead together,' he ordered.

The M.L. slid gingerly over the placid sea for another five miles, picking up the last of the survivors as she went. Not until Beachy Head was abeam to starboard, the cliffs gleaming white in the moonlight, did Wally relax and send the men below. Somehow, when floating on top of a gunpowder keg, it felt better to stay up on deck.

It was now four o'clock in the morning and already the first steely shafts of dawn were streaking the eastern horizon.

'Fall out Action Stations. Go to Cruising Stations, Number One.'

'Aye, aye, sir. Orders for the morning?'

Wally shook his weary head and suppressed a yawn.

'E.T.A. Portsmouth, 0730, Number One. We'll have breakfast off the Nab Tower, weather and Huns permitting. Good night, or rather, good morning!'

Jannaway turned for the bridge ladder.

'And, Number One...'

'Yes, sir?'

'Thank you. Well done.'

'Good night, sir.'

'Good *morning*!'

When M.L. 115 reached the Nab, she found Loasby in 113 waiting by the gate of the boom defence vessel. Since the disappearance of a merchant ship in a gale one night on a C.W. convoy, it had become routine to count those who safely reached Portsmouth.

'Report casualties,' blinked the Senior Officer's Aldis.

'Fourteen survivors, two dead, four seriously wounded. Captain Watler, Master of collier *Pomona,* amongst survivors. Intend proceeding to Haslar landing,' Wally replied.

'Good luck. Sorry to leave you with the thick end,' Peter Loasby flashed back. He was waving his cap from his bridge as Wally steamed past.

'Regret to report damaged bow,' Wally replied. 'Will require dockyard assistance.' He saw Peter Loasby fling his cap down in disgust. The Second M.L. Flotilla was already short enough of boats.

After Wally had pulled astern at full speed, he had manoeuvred to pick up a group of swimmers, amongst them Captain Watler of *Pomona,* at the expense of a deep gash in 115's starboard bow. The Master, however, had been saved to fight another day. When the mine exploded beneath his ship, he had been blown into the coal bunkers for'd. All he could remember was the water coming up about his neck as his ship went down. His hands had been torn to shreds when he had scrambled with animal ferocity up the coal to regain the upper deck. He remembered nothing of this until he had shinned down the rope on to the M.L.'s fo'c's'le. Wally had given the Master his bunk so that he could recover from the shock, but now, as the M.L. slipped gently alongside Haslar's pontoon, Captain Watler had fully recovered his composure as he stepped ashore without assistance.

Wally waited in silence as the Haslar staff quietly took charge of their patients. The sick berth attendants waved, then turned their backs on the little ship, which was already slipping astern down Haslar Creek to berth on Petrol Pier.

# CHAPTER 5

*The Balloon Ships*

'Why have you got to go?'

It was Suzanne who asked the question, and it came as a shock after the long silence between them. Wally had taken the afternoon off and she had joined him again outside the main gate, fearful of what the 'Queen Bee' — the head Wren — might conclude if they were seen too much together. They had walked to Alverstoke and taken the turning down Monkton Road towards the Solent. They at last found a quiet corner which, shielded by the nodding spikes of gorse, was a bed of turf running down to the shingle of Stokes Bay. Wally had spread out his blue raincoat for her to sit on. She sat there, knees clasped by her arms up to her chin, gazing out to sea to where the Isle of Wight lazed beneath the rolling clouds of this beautiful October afternoon.

'Though the M.G.B.s are based on Dover, we'll often be in Pompey,' Wally said as he chewed a strand of grass.

'You haven't answered me,' Suzanne persisted. 'Did Bobby Nye ask you whether you'd join M.G.B. 312 — or were you appointed?' She turned towards him, her black eyes hard and looking through him. There was no smile about her pouting lips, upon which was a trace of lipstick.

'You look adorable like that,' Wally said, trying to change the subject. He bent across to stroke her sleek black hair, but she leant away and tossed her head.

'Sub-Lieutenant Bruce, you still have not answered my question.' Now there was a glimmer of a smile. Wally turned towards this elf-like being crouched at his side. His heart pounded, the ache now a persistent symptom whenever Suzanne was near or in his thoughts. He tickled her ear with the piece of grass.

'Honestly, darling, I was appointed to Nye's flotilla, but he's asked me to understudy his First Lieutenant while 312 is building at Bembridge. I said of course I would.'

'Where's Bembridge, my funny Scottish man?'

'*Scot*, please,' Wally said, laughing.

She had released her knees and now lay on one elbow facing him, her sheer black stockings showing off her shapely legs.

'Why do all French women have gorgeous legs?' Wally asked.

She took his hand and laid it along her cheek.

'You are so droll, *mon cher* Scot… Why do you love me?' she asked quietly. 'I am not beautiful like the others, your beautiful English Wrens.' She kept his hand upon her cheek and turned to look upon this stocky man at her side. He was gazing down at her, his hair touched by the gold of the setting sun. His eyes, now so serious, were bluer than the sea, with the far-away look of the distant Atlantic. Gently he traced the outline of her face with his fingertips.

'I loved you from the moment we talked in Dover, Sukie…' He stumbled for words, unsure of himself. 'When we're apart, it's hell. But that's why Bembridge isn't too bad, is it? It's just over there…' He leant across her to point out the little town at the eastern extremity of the Isle of Wight.

He felt her arm encircle his neck as she gently pulled his face to hers. For the first time she kissed him, her lips so soft, so utterly wonderful… Then, deliberately, she gently pushed him away from her.

'Sukie,' he whispered. 'One day, will you marry me?'

She lay there then, her hands behind her head on the turf, silent and gazing up at the scudding clouds. It was a long time before she answered. Wally sat up, staring across the Solent, unable to look at her.

'No, darling,' she said, talking to the heavens. 'Not yet. You see, I must be sure. It's so soon after...' She faltered, waited, then continued, 'I like you so very, very much, my Scottish man, but I *must* be certain.'

She sat up to be alongside him, then placed her hand on his knee and looked up at him again, gentleness in her black eyes.

'Try to understand, Wally. There are more of my countrymen coming over to join those Submarine Chasers which are being moved to their new base at Cowes. Perhaps I will go with them, yes? This will help to mend my heart and *make* me pull myself together.'

Wally felt a pang of jealousy. Brutally he asked, 'D'you know any of them, then?'

She averted her head and looked away to where a late spike of golden gorse nodded in the breeze. He felt her hand slipping from his knee.

'I knew Gilbert Fragonard, one of the Chaser officers.'

'When, Suzanne?'

'We were at school together.'

Again Wally felt the valley of misunderstanding widening. He asked quietly: 'What's he doing over here?'

'He's the new captain of Chaser 43.'

Wally suddenly knew how ridiculous he was being. He held out his hand to her. She looked away and did not respond.

'Suzanne, I'm sorry,' he said. 'They say you hurt those you love.'

She turned to him.

'Do you really love me, *chéri*?'

He would never forget those questioning eyes, so black and intense, glowing from her pale face with its snub nose and soft, petal lips.

He kissed her on the mouth, then gently brushed his lips against her forehead.

'Enough to marry you, my Sukie...'

She nodded, frightened at the development their friendship was taking. 'You're too impetuous,' she whispered, gently extricating herself from his encircling arms.

'I love you. That's all there is to it. And, you never know... There's a war on.'

She gazed again over the Solent, where a Hunt-class destroyer was working up to her full speed trials across the measured mile. Her eyes reproached him. She picked up her uniform bag and began to get up.

'War is no reason to hasten marriage, Wally. Surely,' she whispered as she turned to trace the outline of his face with her sensitive fingers, 'the *bon Dieu* will preserve you for me if we are meant to become man and wife.'

Wally smiled down at her while he drank in her beauty.

'I'll be waiting for you,' he said, 'should you ever change your mind.'

A shaft of sunlight suddenly broke through the clouds scudding low over the sparkling water. The light swept over the shore, kissed the turf-fringed beach, touched the gorse dancing in the wind.

She smiled up at him, her face serene with a quiet contentment.

'That's a woman's prerogative,' she said as she slipped her arm through his. 'Come on, we'd better get back, Wally. There's the siren... d'you hear it? Over Gosport?'

Portsmouth dockyard was too busy to take M.L. 115 in hand immediately for repairs, so she carried out one further escort duty on a C.E. convoy. Off Dover, Wally received a signal to proceed into dockyard hands at Chatham, so, towed by a balloon ship around the 'Forelands' in order to minimise the danger from acoustic mines, M.L. 115 finally glided alongside No. 3 Jetty in Chatham dockyard. Wally was summoned to the Commander's office to be told he was now officially appointed (additional) to M.G.B. 312 who was undergoing modifications at Woodnutt's yard in Bembridge, Isle of Wight. He was to take passage back to Portsmouth in *Astral*, the Senior Officer's ship of the Mobile Barrage Balloon Flotilla.

This was the manner of Wally's becoming, for one short spell, an honorary member of the elite band of men serving in this unique flotilla. Commanded by Lieutenant-Commander Garth Owles, these ships afforded the convoys and escort the protection of a physical screen, in the form of steel wires suspended from balloons, against the Stukas and M.E. 109s. The flotilla and the ships were manned and handled by naval personnel, but the balloons and their gear were operated by the R.A.F.: hence, in deference to the Junior Service, this motley collection of ships was honoured with the name of 'Squadron' — 952 Squadron.

Wally boarded an R.A.F. launch which took him off to *Astral*, at anchor off Southend. He was taken straight down to the ward room, where the Captain was writing a last-minute report.

'Aha!' he said, looking up and smiling. 'Welcome aboard *Astral*, Bruce. Good morning, you others.'

'Good morning, sir,' said Tony Puckle, a jolly, plump Pilot Officer, R.A.F.

'Have you seen this, sir?' asked Flight Officer Alan Forster, in charge of 'Q' Flight of Balloons. He was tall, sophisticated and self-confident, having been a competent journalist ashore. He always smoked Woodbines which he kept in a dirty old tin with foreign stamps stuck inside the lid. He now pulled out one of the six daily papers he had brought off the shore with him, and pointed to a headline: *RENEWED SHELLING OF DOVER AREA*.

The Commander pursed his lips as if he were savouring a sip of wine. 'Just getting the range again.'

'I'm told they're testing their new barrels; they wore out the old lot last time we went through.'

'Have a slice, Bruce?' said the Commander suddenly. 'You might get the glasses, Dick,' he added, turning towards his Fourth Officer, Dick Addis.

'Well, just the odd touch, sir.'

Wally stowed his gear under the ward room lockers while they had their drinks. It was a marvellous feeling to be accepted so readily by such a close-knit band of men.

The ward room was tiny, as narrow as a railway carriage, and it seemed grossly overcrowded. The Commander sat down, his cap on the back of his head; his face was deeply lined, though he was still a young man. The others were standing. Joe, the Number One, was already wearing seaboots and was standing in the far corner talking with Tony Puckle.

They spoke of bombs and shells and the London raids. Someone let a glass ring, and the Commander leapt up to stop it: it really worried him because of the superstition that, every time a glass was allowed to ring until the sound subsided, a sailor drowned.

Tony looked up and said, 'I see you've got a hospital ship with you this time.'

'That should come in nice and handy,' Addis said. 'All we need is a floating dock and there we are.'

Dick Addis, reserved and taciturn, was Officer of the Watch for the forenoon, and he rose to check that all was well on deck.

Ten minutes later, *Astral* put to sea. Wally was asked by the Captain to understudy Addis, so both Sub-Lieutenants found themselves on the bridge as the ship slipped down on the tide.

There was always some commotion when leaving. Usually the Chief Engineer would come up and say they could not possibly go to sea, or *Pintale* would signal that her capstan had broken down and she could not weigh anchor, but somehow or other they managed to sail at the right time.

*Astral* met the convoy and was soon in formation: the sweepers well ahead, *Astral* next, and the rest of the balloon ships dotted at intervals among the merchantmen, who were strung out a cable and a half apart in their wake. The little M.L.s kept vague station on them, and the two destroyers slunk along, one on either beam of the convoy.

It was a good sight: the dirty coasters, the balloons shining silver as they sailed through the air, the sleek destroyers. The ship's company felt happy, and rather — what was the word? — gallant. Nothing ever happened during the first hour.

Addis lit a cigarette and gave one to Stone, the young signalman who was the third member of the 'staff', together with the Commander and Addis. He always held a cigarette in the palm of his hand and kept it in his pocket between puffs. As a result his palms were stained a deep brown, except when he washed before going ashore.

'What's that ridiculous pink thing you've got on your head?' Addis asked. It was a revolting knitted hat, in the worst shade of crushed strawberry.

Alan Forster walked up and down the deck. The Commander was busy conning the ship. The shore looked misty and blurred. Addis and Wally stayed up for half an hour or so to see if everything was in order, then went below for lunch, leaving Joe, the First Lieutenant, on the bridge. After roast beef and vegetables, cheese and some execrable coffee, Addis and Wally returned to the bridge to relieve him. Luckily visibility was fairly good, and the buoy-to-buoy navigation was child's play, although they had to keep a check on station-keeping. Every now and then, Addis called down a change of revs to the engine room.

About two o'clock they heard the sirens sounding very faintly from across the water — a thin, sad wailing. A few minutes later the M.B.B.'s own base took it up, fairly screaming out the warning, while the dockyard hooter jerked out short, sharp shrieks.

'There goes our signature tune,' said Stone.

The air was clouded with the haze of a cold day. They could see nothing in the sky, and it was not long before the all-clear sounded. The water was dark and oily, and bits of wreckage kept floating by — slimy bales, broken planks, floats, cans, and tangled ropes. Addis trained his glasses on to something; it was the body of a man, very much swollen, drifting along bottom upwards. The masts and funnels of wrecks broke through the tide here and there. Wally had known many of them when they were ships, afloat and alive.

The Commander and the others came up on the bridge and stood gazing back at the convoy with only the helmsman looking ahead. Stone read out a signal flashed from one of the destroyers, something about lowering the balloons. This irked the Captain as they were his pigeon, so they amused themselves inventing rude replies.

The Commodore of the convoy ran up a hoist of flags: 'Form two columns,' said Stone, though he need hardly have bothered: they knew the routine so well. They kept on a steady course and reduced speed while the Commodore bore off to port as guide of his column. The merchantman fussed around, small, smoky and ugly. A black tin can of a ship came surging up astern of them.

'She's coming to lunch again,' said Forster, as the ship forged ahead towards them. Her bows were abreast their bridge by the time she bothered to slow down.

'Stone,' Addis called, 'we really must stop that ship.'

From the other side of the bridge, Addis could hear him droning, 'Oh! What a surprise for the Duce!'

'Stone, I've told you a hundred times, I will not have that song aboard this ship,' said Addis.

'I thought you liked it, sir.'

'If it occurs again I'll give you ten days' cells.'

Nothing abashed, Stone started on 'I haven't time to be a millionaire'.

'I suppose you can sing *that* if you really want to,' Addis said, 'at least it's — aha! Do you hear what I hear?'

There was the thud of gunfire from somewhere at the rear of the convoy.

'Shore practice,' said Stone hopefully.

But Addis saw the black puffs of the bursting shells and there, a good way off, was a dark speck in the sky.

Forster lifted his binoculars.

'Spitfire,' Addis said firmly.

Forster was still looking. 'Well, without much conviction, I'd say it was an ME 110.'

They were just rounding a buoy.

'Starboard easy,' Addis said. 'Steady on south seventy-three east.'

'South seventy-three east she is, sir.'

'Here she comes,' said Forster. 'Where's my tin titfer? *Seldom if ever...*'

Addis lit a cigarette and extracted his notebook. The men were already closed up at the guns; the two Hotchkiss on the wings of the bridge followed the plane round, though it was still too early to open fire. The Oerlikon gunner, ordinary Seaman Lofty Tate, was crouching behind his gun, his shoulder strapped to the crutches.

The plane kept its height while it circled the convoy, then swooped down on their port side. Everyone's guns started to blaze away; the Hotchkiss was firing just beside Addis's ear and Wally smelt the cordite, though he hardly noticed the noise. He was listening to the whine of the plane and the sinister whistling of the wind through her ailerons.

'Steer south seventy east!'

'South seventy east. Aye, aye, sir!'

There was some trouble over the Oerlikon and Lofty looked up with a gesture of despair. He was a fine figure in his tin hat. His number two was very red in the face — Addis believed he was blushing — while the loader, tough and stolid as ever, struggled with the magazine.

The Commander climbed on to a stool to look over the dodger; it was easy to forget how short he was. 'What's the matter?' he shouted.

'It's jammed, sir.'

'Oh, hell!' He hit the rail with his fist. 'Shoot the blighter down, shoot the blighter down!'

They wrestled for a few minutes more and then Lofty held up his hand. All the time the plane was drawing nearer.

Wally saw the bombs leave the plane, just two of them. They came out flat, and then slowly rolled nose downwards. Then the screaming began, shrill and rising horribly. Wally could hear the *woof! woof!* from the destroyers, the rattle of the Hotchkiss and the quick thuds of the Oerlikon. The tracers streamed up towards the plane, some pink, some yellow, some green. The shriek of the bomb was now right inside Wally's head. The quartermaster had his hands on the wheel, but he was not looking at the compass. The Commander was holding his hat on with one hand while he peered up at the plane.

The ship shook as the bombs burst. Wally saw the flash and the smoky fountains of water that seemed to hang in the air. Addis looked at his watch and wrote down in the log: *1548. Two near misses on port beam.*

Sandy, the Hotchkiss gunner, was smiling, his great gums showing.

'Beast!' said Forster.

The plane climbed steeply with the shells bursting all around her, and they thought she was off. But she turned and came back on their starboard side, very low, so that most of the ships could not aim at her.

'I don't like these brave ones,' Addis said.

'He wants to be a hero,' said Stone.

She came so close that Wally could see her pilot. Then she opened up with her guns, with a dull sound like the popping of champagne corks. Wally could see the splashes where the bullets hit the water, long regular lines coming towards them. There were puffs of smoke along the leading edge of her wings. She passed and, quite objectively, they watched her attack one of the ships astern.

'Bad shooting,' said the Commander. She might have killed some men in that other ship, but *Astral* was not hit at all. That was all that mattered for now.

She circled them once more; then, gaining height, made off towards France. Wally watched her idly and was glad she was gone. There were some curious explosions in the water as she passed over. They wondered what on earth they could be, and were inclined to jeer.

Addis wrote down what had happened in his log, lit another cigarette and checked up on the course.

'South seventy-five east,' he said.

'South seventy-five east she is, sir.'

'There goes our messenger to Jerryland,' said Forster.

'That'll just give them time to get the bungs out.'

'What time do we get to the shooting range, Dick?'

'About six-fifteen.'

'The question is, do we eat before or after?'

'Oh, after, I think. It'll be all over by nine o'clock.'

'We hope,' added Stone.

'Hope nothing. "All over" can be taken either way.'

Addis remembered how once, owing to some mistiming, they had arrived hours too early and could see the French coast warping the horizon. He could not wipe from his mind a picture from *Illustrated* of a German officer looking through glasses across the Channel. He thought of him waiting there, of a gun's crew eating their supper so as to be ready for *Astral's* coming, of his harsh voice and of the little smile on his face. It was not a pleasant thought.

It was past four o'clock now, so Joe took over the watch. The Commander and Forster went below, but Wally stayed up for a while.

Joe and Addis sang a little and talked. They'd been seeing many Wild West films lately, so they practised the jargon and remembered how funny Tony Puckle looked in his sheepskin jacket, twirling a pistol in either hand.

At four-thirty the steward came up on to the bridge with tea and buttered toast.

'How did you like the party?' Addis asked.

'I was busy wiping the cat's chin,' he said. 'She wasn't feeling very well.'

He was a most superior man, and could carry five plates of soup at once. They ate some toast, but Wally's hands smelt foul through holding on to the brass rail. His feet were warm and he could move his toes in comfort.

Stone came up with his own tea in a tin mug.

'Have some bu'ered toast,' Addis said. The steward had a real Cockney accent, and they made him recite *I got to get a bit of butter.* 'I go' 'a ge' a bi' o' bu'er,' he said.

The light was failing and they had a last cigarette before darken ship. Addis was glad when darkness came. There would be no moon, which was fortunate.

It was about five-fifteen when, leaving Joe on watch, Addis and Wally went down to the ward room. The Captain was sitting in duffle coat and seaboots, fast asleep, his cap tilted over his eyes, his feet sticking out. Addis climbed round him to the table, took up a pack of cards and began playing Patience. The first time was hopeless, but the second went well, far too well, so he stopped before the end. They had proved it was bad luck to finish a game successfully.

Wally went through the mess room to the heads. Many of the sailors were already sprawled out: some on the tables, some on the settees, some on the deck. All were fully dressed and the room smelt very close.

He came back into the ward room to find Forster there, reading *Esquire,* with the cat on his lap. She was pitch black and had a warty growth behind her left ear. 'Who's the bravest Belgian pussy in the Channel?' he was saying. He looked across at Addis. 'What trip is this, Dick?' he asked.

'The twenty-fifth, I think,' Addis said, fiddling with the cards.

'Well, it's about time you told me; you never let us forget.'

'Beast,' Addis said.

'What about the Ritz Bar in New York?' suggested Forster, 'with a beautiful waitress bringing iced drinks; and sweet music behind the palm trees?'

'Give me Count Basie and a bit of zazz-zu-zazz. And fried sole with oyster sauce.'

They told each other fairy stories like that and then Addis picked up Fothergill's *Innkeeper's Diary* and began reading. It was good to think of Oxford and the river and long evenings in the garden.

'What's the time?' asked Forster.

That was an unpleasant reminder.

'Just time for the news.'

Addis switched on the wireless and they heard the last few minutes of Henry Hall. He was playing A *Nightingale Sang in Berkeley Square*, and Wally thought of Suzanne. Big Ben chimed in and the announcer started the news. He sounded infuriatingly calm, and they felt his voice might drown other sounds — sounds they did not want to hear. They listened to the headlines and then switched off.

'Well?' said Forster, and smiled.

'I'm restless,' Addis said. 'I need cheering up. You can give me a ciggy.'

'That's a revolting phrase. I suppose you want a "lucy" to light it with.'

The Captain was still out to the wide. Wally picked up a *Picture Post* and turned over the pages. The ship was surging on, slowly but relentlessly.

Wally could hear the footsteps of someone coming down the ladder. He looked at his watch: just six-thirteen. There was a knock at the door and their best seaman, a little Manxman, poked his head in.

'Excuse me, sir; the First Lieutenant says either they're blitzing the French coast or else the shelling's begun.'

'All right.'

Addis went over and shook the Commander. 'They've started, sir.'

'Aha!' he said, and was wide awake at once. The ward room was warm and light and friendly. He picked up his tin hat and they followed him out.

# CHAPTER 6

## *All in the Day's Work*

As they went into the alleyway, their old Scottish Leading Seaman passed, his face ingrained with dirt, his lips drawn into his toothless mouth. He was singing in a high, acid voice. In the mess room Wally saw the seaboots of someone stretched out asleep. From the galley came the sound of the cook shifting his pans as he prepared the supper.

At first, Wally and Addis could see nothing as they came out into the darkness. Then, blinking their eyes, they ran up the ladder on to the bridge, their footsteps ringing out aloud. Addis made out a shadowy form on the port wing, and made his way towards it.

'Just in time.'

'Oh, it's you, Joe. Haven't they come yet?'

'Give 'em a chance.'

The coxswain was at the wheel again; the dim light of the binnacle showed up his face, grey and unshaven, with peering eyes. Like a real fisherman he had kicked off his boots and was standing in stockinged feet.

There was a buoy flashing close ahead; it drew so slowly towards them, so slowly. Stone came up the ladder, whistling jauntily; Forster was talking to the Commander. Addis extricated his notebook from his duffle coat pocket and moved over to the starboard side to the chart table with its shaded light.

They waited.

There was a bright blue flash, close ahead; then two more, a little farther off. Then came the sharp, shattering crack of the explosions, not a thick crunch like a bomb. There was no sound of their approach, no warning scream, only the sudden flash and crack in the darkness.

'That'd be about the sweepers,' said the Commander.

Addis wrote: *1814.3 bursts ½ mile ahead.*

Wally could see now: the blurred outline of the headland on the starboard bow and, close to the northward, the ghostly white cliffs. The air was keen and the stars shone, calm and clear.

Now Wally forced himself to look southward. His eyes strained past the ships, trying somehow to pierce the shadows towards Cap Gris Nez. But he wasn't thinking of that hazy coastline he had seen, blue and forbidding, by day; he was watching for the light that must shatter the darkness. Then a tongue of deepest orange fire shot upwards, wonderfully high, and another, and another, and all around was a yellow glow that stayed and hovered in the clouds above.

There were seventy seconds to wait now. The buoy was winking away unmercifully, quite unmoved. He began to count the flashes: one, two, three, and then a pause; one, two, three, endlessly repeated. The English coast looked warm and comfortable, but with this tide they had small chance of swimming ashore.

'We're falling back a bit,' said the Commander.

Joe pulled the plug out of the engine room voicepipe and whistled down: 'Up five.'

'Up five; aye, aye, sir.'

And the shells were still on their way.

That sounded like the Chief down below. He wouldn't hear as much as they did, because these shells burst on hitting the water and spent their fury in the air. Wally wondered what it would be like to be wounded. There would be rest and quiet to follow, but it wouldn't stop the shelling.

Seventy seconds. Wally had been looking at the buoy for such a long time; surely they ought to have come by now? But perhaps he was wrong; perhaps it was just A.A. fire he'd seen, perhaps —

The flash and the crack came almost together, and the sound was devastating; they ducked behind the canvas dodger. The next salvo was louder; the third rocked them with its blast and the smell came to them; the noise was within them and was a physical pain and the air sang with the whirring fragments.

Wally saw the tower of water close on their starboard beam.

'Seldom, if ever...' said Forster, and Stone laughed.

The water sank slowly down and, from out of the midst of it, a little dark shape emerged.

'Poor old M.L.s,' Addis said.

'That nearly made them look pretty silly,' said the Commander.

Wally chuckled in the darkness.

'Can I make that half a cable, sir?' Addis asked, pencil poised.

'It can't have been much more.'

As he wrote it down in his book, Wally saw the glow that told him more were on their way.

'That looks almost like another battery, doesn't it, sir?'

'It did seem to be a bit farther back. Make a note of it, will you? Damn that Commodore! Why can't he keep a steady pace?'

'Down five,' said Joe.

'Down five... aye, aye, sir.'

Forster came over from the other side of the bridge. 'I've never been so frightened. That last lot nearly blew my tin titfer off. How did…'

The salvo burst, about half a mile astern.

'As I was saying when I was so rudely interrupted, how did you enjoy it?' Forster asked.

'I'm rather brave now.' Suddenly Wally felt it was all right; they wouldn't hit *Astral*.

'The Terror of the Channel?'

'Cap'n to you.'

It had begun, and they knew they could stand it now; they had had it all so often. It was only the waiting that was bad.

'Starboard easy,' said Joe. 'Steady south eighty-two west.'

'South eighty-two west she is, sir.'

They passed close to the buoy; Wally could see how large it really was, and the shape of its lantern.

Everything was blue in the darkness; only the binnacle glowed a deep orange. Ships were thronging all around them; they showed no lights, no lights at all, and they were only two cables apart. If they wandered at all off course, they would probably be mined. These men had seen it happen, only too often. Once after a gale, they had had to feel their way through over forty mines that floated, brown, rusty and menacing, in their path.

Then Wally heard the drone of aircraft overhead, and up from England a searchlight felt its way; then another and another till the darkness was latticed with shafts of moving light. The A.A. guns opened up and he could see the white tongues of fire from their muzzles and the flash of their shells bursting in the sky. Yet there was no sound from them.

The wind was cold and Wally's hands were swollen and stiff. Drifts of spray were salt on his lips, but thankfully it was not raining. Forster put the hood of his duffle up and looked like an overgrown and licentious pixie. The searchlights moved out to sea till they were leaning right over *Astral*, to make pools of yellow in the sky above her.

Then Forster called out: 'It looks as if Jerry's getting a caning.'

Wally turned southward, where the French coast was suddenly alive.

There were machine-gun bullets darting up, brilliantly white, and Bofors lobbing up their scarlet slugs; and flaming onions like balls of fire, whilst every now and then a curtain of light exploded from a bursting bomb. But still in the midst of the firework display was that particular glow that told of more shells on their way; that would never stop. Then the enemy searchlights shone out, to arch over the sea; the English and the Germans met and held hands over the Channel. The convoy was steaming along so slowly: such dirty little ships, with gunfire and bombs and shells on either side of them and an arch of searchlights above their heads. It was beautiful and it was terrible.

'Talk about driving a bus through No Man's Land,' Wally said.

'I don't think it slows the shelling much,' remarked the Commander, 'but it slows up the convoy.'

For twenty minutes they sailed in glory; then the lights went out and they were left in the blue darkness, alone with their shelling.

An hour went by and the salvos still came over. The Germans seemed to be raking the convoy from van to rear — or, rather, the enemy would aim ahead of them and keep their guns on that bearing until the convoy had passed, then shift left and start again. Not all the shells fell near the ships, some being several miles short.

'That's almost insulting,' the Commander said, as one landed somewhere in mid-Channel.

'They have to train the beginners sometimes,' replied Joe.

'We ought to get paid as target ships,' Wally said. 'It's damned silly to give it to them free.'

'What's the score to date?'

Wally totted it up in his little book, sticking his head under the canvas flap to get at the light. 'Blast! We never noticed the century. It's now 124, not counting the lot that never arrived.'

'Those must have been incredibly short; I never heard a thing.'

By eight o'clock they had passed the 200. Three-quarters of an hour or so before, Stone had produced the theory that each shell cost £600 (he swore he had read that somewhere), so they had fun reckoning up the bill to Hitler, and ordinary things became highly amusing. They vied with each other in spotting the fall of shot; they took off their tin hats; they talked and laughed and were happy to be together.

There were just seven of them on the bridge: the Commander, Forster, Joe, Stone, the Quartermaster, Addis and Wally. All around them was the black sea and the night, the mysterious forms of other ships and those sudden, fantastic explosions. But the men on the bridge were real and alive. They had all done this so many times; they were all so carefully poised that nothing they said or did would jar any of the others, or tumble him off his particular stand and support. They knew each other, stripped and naked, and they were as brothers.

They were not excited now. They were silent, not bored, but flat and drained of energy. There was no novelty, no heroics; there was just an irksome and long-drawn-out job to be done.

They were proud, vastly proud, though their pride took a curious form. They knew that the cargo they brought through was immaterial to them; they knew that the escort was out of all proportion to the merchant ships; they knew they were doing little to win the war; all that they knew. They never spoke of 'Hell's Corner'; they were not so very efficient or alert; they referred to 'Churchill's Channel' when they were having a particularly unpleasant time; they laughed sardonically when they read in the papers of 'Big Guns in Channel Duel.' But they gloried in their futility. They felt — and discussed among themselves — that they must be hit sooner or later, that only a few might survive, and they were all the closer and all the prouder for this thought. It was not everybody who could cock a snook at Hitler twice a week.

Nothing had fallen at all close to them for some while now. It was sometimes difficult to keep count of the bursts, and Wally could not always tell how many were on their way, which flashes were — so to speak — overdue. Most of the shells seemed to be falling well astern, but it was impossible to say how far. They had not consciously marked the strain before, but they felt the relaxation now; they began for the first time to think of the next few hours and to hope for a quiet night. Wally noticed how cold it was and the roll of the ship; he felt the dirt of his hands and the rough warmth of his coat.

'You know, Joe,' Addis said, 'after the war, we must do a trip through the Channel with all our lights blazing out and the buoys as bright as Piccadilly Circus. We'll smoke on deck, open all the scuttles and flash signals about like mad. We'll have a balloon, of course, and all the officers will man the ship — all right, I suppose Stone'll have to come — and we'll get Brocks to stage a terrific firework display, just so that we'll feel at home.'

'*Pintale*'s funnel is a good enough Roman candle on its own; just look at her now. But you'd far better come on a P and O cruise with me.'

'Will you still speak to me when you're first mate of the *Strathnaver*?'

It was a quarter to nine and they were weary, cold and hungry. Ahead, Wally could just make out the buoy that marked what was usually the end of the 'shooting range'. Addis hardly bothered to write down anything now. For five minutes nothing had come, for ten, for fifteen.

'The party seems to be over,' said the Commander. 'Let's go and get some food.'

Addis closed his book.

'You go down, Dick,' said Joe. 'Take Bruce with you and relieve me when you've finished.'

'Is that O.K. by you? I warn you, we'll be hours, and probably drink ourselves silly.'

'Just you try.'

It was warm in the ward room, and there were cigarettes and gin, bacon, eggs and chips. The Commander was in his best form, telling long, glorious stories and laughing in his own magnificent way, shouting, shameless and happy. But Addis and Wally could not linger, for Joe was waiting.

Wally liked this watch. They were tired after the excitement, but they were at peace, and loved the ship and the keen air and the sea. Stone came up with mugs of cocoa, thick and greasy and very hot, and they talked of many things, knowing each other so well. They finished and Addis sent him below to turn in. Addis could do any signalling that was necessary.

A few planes hummed overhead, and a forest of searchlights greeted their coming before the aircraft disappeared. There were always strange things happening: pyrotechnics from German planes identifying themselves to their own ships; muffled, unexplained explosions; sudden, strange noises. Addis noted them all down. One entry read simply: *2113. Apparently the Royal Scot passed over ship.* It was all Addis could say; nothing else could describe that rushing, shattering roar, though what the cause was they could not imagine. Once some parachute flares were dropped; the cloak of darkness was stripped away, and they were left alone and naked in that cruel brilliant light. It was a dream world.

Joe came up, and they stayed and talked for some time before they went below to sleep, fully dressed, lying on the settees.

At four o'clock, Addis and Wally were on watch again for the morning watch. They had only just settled with their mugs of cocoa when the port lookout shouted abruptly: 'Listen, sir!'

Then suddenly, above the sound of the wind in the rigging and the swish of the sea slapping against the sides, came the sound of a motor boat's engines on their port bow. The boat was distinctly audible because *Astral* was drifting, her engines stopped, as she waited on the port bow of the convoy for it to catch up.

'Listen,' Wally said. 'She's run up her engine twice in neutral. Now she's crossing our bows.'

There was a low *thrum, thrum of* engines and then the sound vanished into the night.

Lieutenant-Commander Owles was alert on *Astral*'s bridge, but with the Aldis signalling lamp broken down since leaving the Downs, there was little he could do. Then, five minutes later, came the explosion they had all been dreading. A few seconds later another, with a bright flash lighting up the sky astern. Evidently the two torpedoes must have found the same target.

'Poor blighters,' Addis whispered. 'They hadn't a chance.'

Then the night lit up: scarlet tracers and green, intermixed and curling through the darkness.

'A proper Brock's Benefit,' the Captain muttered. 'Waste of ammo. No one knows who's firing at whom.' He paused as he peered through his binoculars. 'We'll remain where we are, Sub. Pass the word: I'll court-martial anyone who opens fire. We'll stay dead quiet and hope the E-boats don't see us.'

*Astral* drifted silently in the darkness, as did her opposite number, M.B.B. *Borealis* and the cargo ship, *Empire Crusader.*

'There's nothing we can do,' Addis said sympathetically to his Captain.

'Thanks, Sub. No, there's not much we could do with our feeble armament. We'd better let the escort fight it out.'

The battle raged for another twenty minutes, the British M.T.B.s putting up a blanket of fire as they charged up and down the convoy, the little M.L.s darting in and out and fussing like elderly aunts. There was a hiss, a *phew-w-w*, through the air close astern, but nothing exploded or found its mark.

'Wish the M.T.B.s wouldn't use those flares,' said the Captain. 'Makes us stand out like a house.'

Then gradually the firework party fell astern and those on the bridge of *Astral* breathed again. Their relief was short-lived as, slap on their port beam, two white flares shot high into the sky to come floating down as slowly as thistledown. Night became as light as day, with *Borealis* and *Astral* standing up like battleships, their balloons flying, silvery orbs, high in the night sky.

'Dammit,' the Captain muttered. 'They must have a destroyer well to seaward; she's lobbing starshell over the convoy. Some of the E-boats must be inshore of us; they're lighting up the sky with flares.'

'Too easy for the rest of the E-boats,' Addis said. 'They're picking us off like flies.'

There was a crash in the night and a shower of flame and sparks astern of them.

'Must be *Borealis*,' Addis said.

They felt sickened because their sister ship had caught the torpedo, but in the flash that followed she was still there, floating and upright, her balloon above her.

'No, it must be *Holme Force* or one of the escorts,' the Captain said. 'They're the only other two ships in that position.'

The tension on the bridge was electric as all eyes strained to catch the first glimpse of an attacking E-boat — the splash of a torpedo or the murderous raking of machine-gun fire was all they could see from *Astral*.

'There she is!' the starboard lookout shouted, hand outstretched, as a further burst of machine-gun fire spluttered to starboard. It was the escort, and the fire from the British M.T.B.s was now distinguishable. They were shooting upwards, but the E-boats, having fired torpedoes, were blazing downwards at the bridges of the small ships, raking them from stem to stern.

'Wonder how many of us have been sunk,' the Captain mused aloud.

They never found out. The night wore on as everyone waited for the next attack. But no attack came, and then the darkness thinned, the horizon reddening and growing more distinct.

After breakfast they all came up on the bridge and contentedly watched the familiar coastline. One of the other balloon ships flashed a signal.

'What was that, Stone?'

He handed Addis the pad. 'From *Borealis: Sub killed. Number One seriously injured.*'

Wally heard the story afterwards. They were all up on the monkey's island, the Captain and his two officers. It was almost the last salvo, when they had remarked, 'There's nothing more to bother about,' when they had said, 'the party's over.' A splinter flew (such a small hole it made in the canvas screen), and went through the Sub's head, while another smashed the First Lieutenant's leg. There was a very steep ladder up, and it was impossible to get either of them down. The Captain was left there all night, with one dead man and one bleeding to death. The Sub had been writing at the chart table at the time; he had just put down *2048. 3 flashes on the French coast.* It was those shells that killed him. Seventy seconds is a long time to wait.

Addis had often sailed in that ship. He remembered the Sub, very young and nervous and very brave. He remembered how the Sub had taken the wheel in that amazing gale when all the crew were sick, and the Captain and Addis had stood all night on the open bridge, singing, 'Are you happy in your work? Sure we are.' The Sub was a great chap.

Still the convoy plodded onwards, now making little way, with the strong spring tide against them. The Isle of Wight was visible now, St Catherine's Point, the lighthouse and the green fields inland.

Wally breathed a sigh of relief — they had counted only six balloon ships still afloat, including themselves and *Borealis*, now visible in the early sunlight astern. The Hunt-class destroyers

*Bulldog* and *Beagle* were threshing backwards and forwards, trying to gather up the remnants of what had once been a convoy and which was now, to all intents and purposes, non-existent.

'There's *Gatenais*!' Addis shouted. There was a cheer from those on the bridge. *Gatenais* was the seventh balloon ship; they were all safe. It was difficult not to feel pleased over one's own. Many men had died the night before, but it was still possible to be glad that one's friends had survived — and difficult, too, not to reproach oneself for this callousness.

The telephone shrilled from aft.

'Captain here…'

'Permission to top up, sir?' asked Pilot Officer Puckle, the R.A.F. officer on duty at the balloon aft. This would mean *Astral* steaming on ahead of the convoy, so that she could stop for the topping-up operation to be carried out on the balloon. The convoy would then catch up again with *Astral* in approximately her correct station.

'I think I'll wait till later in the forenoon,' the Captain replied. 'I'll know a bit more then.'

'Aye, aye, sir,' Puckle's voice came faintly.

'But haul down to 300 feet, Tony,' the Captain ordered. 'Cloud base is now only 300 feet.'

'Aye, aye, sir.'

So the work of the balloon ships went on, day in, day out; unglamorous, routine… yet the convoys dared not sail without the M.B.B.s, with their bulbous monstrosities swinging high above from their invisible steel wires.

At ten o'clock, aircraft were seen circling high overhead. *Astral* went to Action Stations, but with no Aldis lamp it was impossible to know whether the aircraft were friendly.

'Wish to goodness I knew what was going on,' Lieutenant-Commander Owles said. 'We must have two signalling lamps in the future, Signalman.'

'Aye, aye, sir.'

'I don't know how we stand; I can't talk to anyone, and we look like getting another basinful tonight.'

By 1130, *Astral* had moved ahead of the convoy and topped up her balloons with gas. Only twenty-five minutes later there was no mistaking the cloud of aircraft hovering over the convoy: about thirty Stukas, with a couple of Messerschmitt squadrons as escort.

'Alarm red-two-o, angle of sight eight-o,' the Captain said calmly. 'Better take that lot, Number One. They'll go for our balloons first.'

By now the remaining ships in the convoy had added their firepower to that of the escort. The whole convoy was blazing away as the ME 109s swooped down on the balloons, which folded into flaming streamers of fabric as the guns of the fighters clattered overhead; then, like one platoon following another on the parade ground, the Stukas plummeted downwards upon the convoy. In their vertical dives, with their wing sirens screaming, with their guns spitting and their irresistible precision, these JU 87s were a terrifying and implacable foe.

The Commodore of the convoy, *Empire Crusader,* was struck immediately; enveloped in bomb splashes, with flames leaping upwards, she was smashed from stem to stern. As Wally turned his agonised gaze away, he saw *Whitley*, a small tramp, jerk suddenly, then her bridge mushroomed into flame. Soon she heeled over to port, hovered a moment and began to sink, her rust-splotched bottom rolling upwards as she went.

'My God, sir!' Addis shouted. 'Poor old *Borealis* has caught it!'

All on the bridge spun round: *Borealis* was their 'chummy' ship and they knew each other well, warts and all. Her starboard bow was cut by a huge hole and her bridge was ablaze, with tongues of orange flames leaping upwards through the clouds of black smoke.

'Alarm port, sir…'

*Astral's* machine guns stuttered down the length of her side, but the fighters streamed through. Wally could see the underbelly of the 109 as it streaked at masthead height immediately above his head. The leading edge of the fighter's wings spat fire, and then their balloon sparked into flames as it went up.

'Full ahead,' the Captain ordered calmly. 'Reel in the wires, Tony, I don't want them around my screws.'

The whine of the winches right aft was audible even above the racket, as *Astral* twisted and turned from the bombs raining down upon them. 'The Owl', as the Captain was affectionately known, ruggedly stood his ground as he conned the ship to evade the plunging bombs.

'Look, sir,' Addis shouted, 'the bombers are shearing off.'

There was a loud cheer from aft as a couple of Hurricanes stormed over at masthead height, hard on the tail of a Junkers 88. There was a black puff, a slick of smoke, and then the twin-engined fighter spiralled into the sea five hundred yards from *Astral.*

'Let 'em drown,' someone shouted. 'The bastards!'

'We'd better start rescue operations, Tony,' the Captain said. 'Stand by the seaboat.'

The battle was over as quickly as it had begun. The convoy's old Anson appeared from nowhere, her wings dipping to mark the spot where survivors were struggling for their lives. Two more fighters had been shot down, but this was little recompense for the damage the enemy had inflicted on C.W. 93.

The area south of St Catherine's Point was littered with the remnants of the convoy. The balloon ship *René le Besnerais* had already lifted her skirts and was steaming hard with her balloon for 'F' buoy and the Nab Tower. *Elan II* had stopped alongside *Borealis* and had already passed her hawsers to take her in tow.

'Stand by to pick up survivors, port side-to,' Addis telephoned to the quarterdeck. '*Elan*'s seaboat is coming alongside with *Borealis*'s survivors.'

*Astral* shuddered as her engines trundled astern.

'*Pingouin* is doing her stuff, sir,' Puckle said. 'She's trying to take *Empire Crusader* in tow.'

'The whole balloon flotilla's doing its stuff,' the Captain said. 'But if *Crusader* survives the onslaught of *Pingouin*, she'll survive the war…'

*Borealis* was sinking fast, but *Elan II* was still persevering. *Astral* closed the sinking *Whitley* who after all proved to be the Norwegian, *Tres*. Her bridge was wrecked and her hold was raging with flame and smoke.

'She'll never make it,' the Captain said. 'The fire has got too much of a hold to take her in tow.'

Wally looked towards the island. The tide had turned now and they were slowly moving up towards Culver and the safety of St Helens. They took off *Tres*'s wounded by boat and, as they drew clear, *Elan II*'s tow parted from *Borealis*. *Astral* closed rapidly to help but, as she seemed happy, the Captain decided to return to Portsmouth at full speed with *Borealis*'s wounded, who were terribly mutilated.

At 1615 they met a Dutch *schuyt* under tow from a Danube-class seagoing tug.

'I think I'll follow,' the Owl said. 'She knows her way around here. I hate wandering about outside the swept channels.'

So, at 1845, *Astral* secured alongside the destroyer *Acheron* on North Wall in Portsmouth dockyard. The wounded were lifted ashore into the ambulances.

'Sub-Lieutenant Bruce, sir?'

'Yes, Bunts, what is it?'

'Signal for you, sir.'

The signalman saluted. He held out the pad for Wally to read.

*Immediate,* the signal commanded. *Report to M.G.B. 312 forthwith.*

# CHAPTER 7

*The Hornet's Sting*
*St Vaast, Winter 1941/42*

'One-two-six ?... *Heave!*'

Wally Bruce stood below the hull of M.G.B. 312 and listened to the imprecations from the upper deck some twenty feet above him. He waited there a moment, his blue eyes amused and crinkled at the corners from peering up-sun; he stood holding his canvas grip in one hand, the other grasping the rung of the ladder which led up to the gunboat's upper deck. Lying in her cradle on the slipway, her hull, with her smooth, underwater shape, gleamed from the anti-fouling which glistened in the pale sunlight of the November afternoon. He felt elated, at long last on his way to offensive operations against the enemy. He had been appointed supernumerary to Motor Gun Boat 312 in order to understudy and to gain experience. After a month or so, he would have a boat of his own and now he longed to get to sea.

Robert Nye, whom Wally had first met at Dover on his return from Dunkirk, was 312's captain, a light-hearted officer who had been commissioned before the war in the Royal Navy. He had left the service but had now rejoined as an R.N.V.R. Lieutenant. Tall and fair-haired, with sad, amused eyes, he was rumbustious and a born leader, as Wally soon discovered when he gained the gunboat's deck. Nye and another man in their shirt sleeves and braces were wrestling with a circular pad of half-inch steel which they were lining up with the holes bored through the deck. Wally saluted and endeavoured to introduce himself.

'Sub-Lieutenant Bruce, sir, reporting on board to join—'

'Again,' the fair-haired officer gasped, beads of perspiration trickling down his weather-beaten face. 'Lift… one-two-six… He heaved on the bar with which he was levering the base plate of a gun-mounting into position. 'That's it… *now*, Number One, drop in the first bolt.'

The lean and angular First Lieutenant, Roger Lloyd, inserted a long bolt, tapped it and, with a grin, watched it slide neatly into place.

'That's it, sir. The rest'll be easy.'

Both men relaxed from their efforts and, for the first time, noticed Wally.

'Ah — welcome aboard, Bruce.' Robert Nye, eyes summing up the arrival, extended his grimy hand. 'Sorry to greet you like this, old boy, but we've just got our new gun.'

It was later that Wally learnt the story of this unusual armament modification. Bobby Nye, for so he was affectionately known throughout the Fourteenth M.G.B. Flotilla, had finally despaired of acquiring any adequate armament. Piles of correspondence to officialdom still failed to produce results in his running battle with bureaucracy. A bitterness had crept into Coastal Forces because of the lack of appreciation by the men in Admiralty of the terrible consequences of being inadequately armed against the E-boats. Though Ivor Hitchens, the dashing leader of the M.G.B. fraternity, had almost despaired of any results, Bobby Nye had finally managed to 'rabbit' this Rolls Royce 2-pounder gun from an undisclosed source. Woodnutt's, this splendid family yard in Bembridge, had looked the other way when Bobby had requested the loan of drills and tools. So it was that M.G.B.

312, a 'C' class Fairmile, was finally launched from Woodnutt's yard, to be followed by M.G.B.s 324 and 333.

The fitting of the Rolls gun changed the events of 312's life. The Rolls was mounted aft, and with a 2-pounder pompom for'd, two 0.5-inch machine guns amidships, and smoke canisters and depth charges, 312 was heavy, her speed sacrificed for fire power. Because of trials on the Rolls Royce gun and the three supercharged Hall Scott engines, 312 was late in commissioning. Bobby Nye was eventually to become Senior Officer of the First Division of the Fourteenth M.G.B. Flotilla, but now, under the S.O., Lieutenant-Commander W. G. Everitt, R.N., in 316 and with the rest of the flotilla coming later, they worked together on detached operations whenever they were not required for routine patrols with the motor torpedo boats in the Channel.

It was almost three weeks, well into November 1941, before Bobby Nye had worked up 312 to the efficiency he required. At the end of one long day of engine trials, he put into Cowes for the night.

Wally walked to the Chaser base in Artic Road to call upon the Senior Officer, Lieutenant Malcolm Buist, that upright and amusing man whom he had come to know so well when the Chasers were based at *Dolphin*. Buist was not in his office, so Wally strolled down to the foreshore to look for him. It was now dark and he almost collided with two figures walking towards him, one — the smaller of the two — obviously being a Wren. When they saw Wally, the girl shyly extricated her arm from that of her companion.

*'Puis-je vous aider?'* the French *Lieutenant de Vaisseau* asked brusquely.

*'Merci,'* Wally replied. 'I was just looking for Lieutenant Buist.'

'He's at sea,' the Frenchman said. 'What is your name, please?'

Wally felt the hackles bristling on the back of his neck, but before he could reply, the Wren interrupted quietly:

'You're Sub-Lieutenant Bruce, aren't you?'

Wally's heart leapt. As soon as he'd seen these two in the darkness, he had wondered where Suzanne was, and now the lilt in her soft voice was music in his ears.

'Yes, Suzanne, it's me. How are you?'

There was an awkward silence. Then the girl stepped back to introduce her companion.

*'Permettez-moi d'introduire —'* and she turned to look at her escort *'— Lieutenant de Vaisseau Gilbert Fragonard.'*

The Frenchman saluted but did not return Wally's proffered hand. As he turned away, he said in perfect English, 'I see you know each other. I'll wait for you, *chérie,* at the gate.'

Suzanne neither moved nor replied.

'I did not expect to meet you here,' Wally said awkwardly. 'How are you?'

'Quite well, thank you… and you?' Her voice was strained, her words disjointed with embarrassment.

'We can't talk here,' Wally blurted impatiently. 'Can you see me tomorrow? We've got a make-and-mend.' A make-and-mend was a half-day off duty.

'If you wish. But where, Wally?'

'At the bus stop in the centre of the town. About twelve-thirty.' He felt the old ache returning, his pulse quickening. 'I'll bring sandwiches and we'll take a bus into the country. O.K.?'

She hesitated a moment, then laid a hand on his sleeve. Her reply was barely audible. 'I'm very busy tomorrow. Are you sure you want to waste your time with me?'

Wally took her hand in his. He felt the warmth, but there was no response to his touch as he replied: 'Tomorrow it is, then. Twelve-thirty.'

They boarded a bus to Newport, where they changed for another to Alum Bay. They spoke little, apart from banal conversation, until they reached the end of the trip at Totland where they dismounted.

It was one of those soft November afternoons, with the last autumnal golds and browns of the falling leaves clinging to the belief that autumn had not yet departed, Wally stood motionless for a moment, staring down at the Needles Channel far below them, that strip of silver water where he had experienced so much.

'Look, Wally... look at those reds and golds in the bramble leaves.'

Suzanne stood with her hands in the pockets of her heavy uniform greatcoat, which hung halfway down her legs. Her eyes were drinking in the beauty of the afternoon, absorbing the soft colours, relishing the scrub which fringed the cliff edge to where the pastel lines of the sandy cliffs began. The sun glimmered to cast a pale runnel of shimmering light across the water to the west of The Needles.

'If we're to reach Tennyson's Cross before dark, we'd better get cracking, young woman.' Wally held out his hand and, once she had shyly accepted it, began scrambling up the path leading to the crest of Tennyson Down. The chalky track smeared their footwear with white streaks, so that when they had reached the cliff top overlooking the Channel, their uniform shoes were in a mess.

Suzanne shook her head and laughed. 'Whatever will Ma'am say when I get back to base?' For a moment she was her old self: natural, vivacious, gay. Wally threaded his arm through hers and, side by side, they stood motionless to peer over the eight-hundred-foot cliff.

She looked up at the man standing beside her. His mind was suddenly barred to her, his thoughts away over the Channel to where the path of the sun glimmered across the sea that undulated far below them, a silver mirror of unusual calm.

'That's a narrow stretch of water,' he murmured, 'but it makes all the difference.'

His hair was ruffled by the heady breeze wafting across the turf and thyme which sprang softly beneath their feet. His ginger eyebrows jutted fiercely above those piercing blue eyes which, all of a sudden, were withdrawn into his own private world. His freckled face was stern, his cheekbones forming a ridge where his jaws clenched and where, in the hollow of his cheek, there pulsed a nerve. Suzanne remained still, watching him: the man was only twenty, yet already bore the marks of suffering. Though he was only five-foot-six, she still barely reached his shoulder.

'See those rocks off Freshwater?' he said quietly, pointing downwards to their left where the gulls circled, mewing and screaming as they wheeled on the updraughts, hundreds of feet below. 'That's where *Acheron was* mined,' he said. 'December last year.'

She was silent, waiting for the dam to burst. For over a minute they stood still, the cries of the gulls the only sound above the soft breeze.

'It was a filthy night last year when I was lying at Yarmouth. A full gale was blowing when *Acheron* went up. Someone ashore saw the flash. By the time we got there, there was no sign, not a trace in those seas — anyway, we were slap in the middle of our own minefield by then.'

'Any survivors?' Suzanne whispered.

He shook his head and turned away. She slipped her arm around his waist. He took her head and laid it gently on his shoulder. He stroked her cheek as she leant there, his heart pounding beneath her hand.

'How does your mother bear all this?' she asked, not looking up. 'It must be hard for her, on her own.'

'She misses Dad, I think. If he'd been here to share it with her, it wouldn't be so bad.'

'What happened to your father?'

'Killed in Palestine — long time ago. I can't remember him.'

She clasped her arm around him and felt his hand enfolding hers. If only he would speak; only allow the words to rush in a torrent from him; if only he could be less self-conscious, share his inner feelings. These British were a strange people.

'Come on, Sukie,' he said quietly, 'or we'll miss our bus back.'

The sun was already low on the horizon by the time they reached the granite cross which marked the highest point of the Downs. They stood peering at the inscription which told of the Victorian poet laureate who had strode these downs to gain his inspiration.

'His home is less than a mile away: "Faringford". That's where he composed *Crossing the Bar*. He must have been up here when he wrote it. Look, you can see the Shingles from here.'

A line of white was gently curling, slow and heaving, across the banks to the west of The Needles Channel.

'The poem was in honour of his friend, Hallam, who had died. We had to learn it at school.'

'Say it.' She stood close to him, wondering, drawn to this many-sided Scotsman.

'It's sad, dreadfully sad. He wrote a lot about the sea:

*'Sunset and evening star,*
*And one clear call for me!*
*And may there be no moaning of the bar,*
*When I put out to sea...*

'I forget how it goes on… Tennyson was a remarkable man,' Wally went on hurriedly, embarrassed by his eloquence. 'His grandson was a Snotty with me.'

The track led downwards now, along the cliff tops to Freshwater Bay. They halted at a stile set between a clump of gorse bushes.

'Look,' he said. 'There's still some gorse.' A glimpse of gold nodded joyfully in the breeze.

Suzanne smiled, happy to see the slow grin beginning to soften his face. He was looking up at her where she stood upon the wooden step. He held up a hand for support.

'Know what they say in Scotland about the gorse?'

She shook her head.

*'It's kissing time when the gorse is out.'*

'And when is it out, Wally?'

'All the year round. We're no fools north of the border.'

Wally felt the world spinning round him as she came into his arms. He saw her face below him, the wind ruffling her wisps of hair. He leant his face towards hers but, as he did so, he felt her drawing away from him. Her hands came up to push gently against his shoulders.

'No, Wally,' she whispered. 'You mustn't.'

He felt an irrational anger mounting inside him. He jerked away when he heard the diesel engine of the last bus coming down the road from the far side of the village.

'Dammit, girl, I want to marry you,' he blurted. 'Can't you understand?' His voice suddenly fell, remorse creeping into his pleading. 'Sukie, I love you, my darling. Will you marry me?'

He would never forget the look of anguish on her face as she hurriedly donned her cap. She was crying, but remained calm and self-possessed.

'I can't, my dear, funny Scottish man,' she whispered. 'I love Gilbert too, you see. He's one of my own countrymen. He has asked me to marry him too.'

She stepped over the stile. Wally watched the little figure running down to stop the green bus which was now lurching around the corner. He'd love her all his life, but God, how it hurt!

He pulled himself together, rushed after her and jumped aboard. The bus jolted, the engine shuddered and they were away.

Suzanne pointed out of the window. 'Look,' she whispered. 'There's the cross, high in the sky—'

Against the angry red sunset, Tennyson's Cross stood lonely, serene, inviolate, a watcher across the Channel.

'Whenever I see it,' Wally said, 'I'll think of you.'

She squeezed his hand and, in the darkness of the bus, gently pecked his cheek.

The furious activity of the next two months was the best medicine that could have been prescribed for Sub-Lieutenant Walter Bruce. After M.G.B. 312 had completed her trials and her work-up period, she joined the First Division of the Fourteenth Flotilla. Lieutenant-Commander W. G. Everitt, R.N., was Senior Officer of the Division, in M.G.B. 316; Bobby Nye was in 312 and Lieutenant D.M.C. Curtis, R.N.V.R. was in 314.

Everitt had wasted no time. Before Christmas of 1941 had come and gone, the First Division had been carrying out harassing raids on the enemy's coast of occupied France. In between routine anti-E-boat patrols, the First Division had carried out raids on Merlimont, Hardelot-Plage, Dives, Courcelles, St Aubin and Tréport.

After intensive planning by C-in-C Portsmouth and after considerable working-up for the forthcoming operation, Lieutenant-Commander Everitt led his 1st Division silently out of Spithead one evening in the early days of January 1942. Waiting in the dusk in St Helen's Roads off Bembridge were two L.C.P.s — the small wooden landing craft that were used to transport personnel on assault operations — loaded with commandos. 312 and 314 took the L.C.P.s in tow and then the force proceeded at 18 knots, in arrowhead formation across the Channel, 312 and 314 on either quarter of their Senior Officer in 316.

It was a moonless night, the wind Force 4 from the south-west and visibility poor. It was difficult to distinguish the horizon from the sea and, crouched as an extra lookout in the port wings, Wally felt the butterflies of fear fluttering in his stomach, in spite of all the work that had already been carried out for this raid on St Vaast.

Bobby Nye settled down to the night's work, having checked his course and position after leaving F buoy off St Catherine's. He had glanced across to where 314 was bucking just clear of 316's wake.

'Set course for Barfleur light, Number One. We've got a tricky one tonight.'

'Aye, aye, sir.'

Number One dipped below into the dim light of the chart table at their feet. The parallel ruler squealed and a moment later his head reappeared.

'Course, sir, o-six-five.'

The Captain turned to Wally. 'Take her, will you, please, Bruce, while I check tonight's operation.'

Wally took over the boat, the Cox'n silently carrying out his duties as he spun the wheel of the careering craft. Wally was already feeling confident of his abilities in these splendid little boats: he had learnt to think fast and to leave behind any pre-conceived ideas of a 'big-ship' Navy.

'It'll be a change raiding St Vaast,' Nye said above the clamour of the wind and the slap of the waves against their hull. 'It's probably the most difficult of all so far. It's a rotten entrance, and we're required to bring back some Germans — dead or alive.'

There was a momentary lull in the conversation.

'What for?' Number One then asked. 'I like to keep 'em at a distance.'

'I gather our boffins want to know what makes a squarehead tick: his clothes, what they live on — that sort of thing,' Nye said.

'That's why we've got so many of our Commando friends with us, is it?' Number One asked. 'They look like walking arsenals.'

'Shouldn't like to meet 'em on a dark night. Unfriendly,' Wally added. Commandos were a bloodthirsty lot. Not only did they carry Tommy-guns, but they were festooned with hand grenades, revolvers, toggled cheese wire and the standard issue blue-steel poniard.

'You'll have to slip the L.C.P. smartly,' Nye added. 'They won't want to waste much time ashore.'

'Aye, aye, sir — and they'll be coming off in a hurry.'

'Dead right. See the hands are told and tell 'em to get their heads down. This could be a lively night.'

It was the waiting that Wally disliked most in this type of warfare. Cape Barfleur should be picked up at midnight, and that was in three hours' time. He wedged himself into the wings and tried to sleep where he crouched.

The noise of the large battle ensign flapping in the slipstream, the halyards slapping against the mast, formed a background to the swish of the seas, as the three darkened boats scythed their way across the Channel. No lights, not even a blue stern light, betrayed their presence, for soon they would be in the enemy convoy lanes. Yet Curtis in 314 was keeping perfect station, his bow wave a slash of gleaming whiteness in the night.

Wally smiled to himself in the darkness. He'd come a long way and learnt much with Bobby Nye. This dashing captain was someone upon whom he could mould himself. Nye was a born leader, an extrovert, but in action he was as cold as ice, with a detached professionalism. So many of these M.G.B. and M.T.B. officers were like that. A year in the Channel was leaving its own stamp upon them and breeding its own race. Professionalism — yes, that was it.

Except for sleep, they'd had no time off since leaving Woodnutt's at Bembridge. He wondered what Suzanne was doing now — ashore with Fragonard, no doubt. Wally wished that the thought of her didn't still cause an ache in his heart. He loved her, dammit, but there wasn't a chance now. He couldn't fight back, because a squabble with a French ally could cause nothing but harm — even if he won Suzanne. Only time could heal.

The visibility had shut down to about two miles and it was now very dark. Wally's thoughts wavered to his new life in M.G.B.s. Jannaway, whilst waiting for their boat, M.G.B. 336, to be completed, had temporarily joined *Albrighton,* a 'Hunt' class destroyer. Perhaps after tonight's trip, Nye might recommend Wally as experienced enough to take up his new boat… but the waiting seemed interminable.

'Barfleur lighthouse fine on the port bow, sir.'

It was the port lookout, with eyes like a cat, who saw the tall pinnacle, with its attendant dwarf tower, emerging spear-like from the low-lying foreshore.

Wally jammed his binoculars to his eyes. His heart raced as Nye reduced speed to conform with 316, who had already eased down.

'Silent engines,' the Captain snapped.

Wally felt the forward surge as the boat wallowed down into the trough of the seas off the race. He could now see the dark foreshore and the white sheen of the waves where they broke upon the jagged outcrop of rocks which waited to trap the unwary off Barfleur. He could make out the squat tower of the church, and from pre-war he remembered the rock upon which William the Conqueror, the last invader, had set foot in order to board his ship for England.

All hands now waited at their Action Stations, the lookouts tense as they searched the horizon for offshore patrols.

'We're not going in if we run across anything,' Nye said. 'Fixing our position is difficult enough as it is.' He turned to his First Lieutenant crouched over the chart table. 'Where'd that fix put us, Number One?'

'Two miles from Tatihou Island, sir. We're about half a mile to seaward of our line.'

Visibility had dropped down to a mile and it was difficult to pick the Redoute de Réville.

'Keep a lookout and listen for the whistle buoy right ahead,' Nye said quietly. 'Once the Senior Officer finds that, we'll be all right. He won't like swinging down on the tide with these rocks about.' He glanced across at 316's and 314's silhouettes looming now only fifty feet away. 'Stop both.'

M.G.B. 314 drifted up on their Senior Officer's starboard quarter. Everitt leant over his bridge rail and spoke quietly to Curtis who, Wally could see, was grinning in the darkness.

'All set, Dunstan?' Everitt asked.

'Ready, sir.'

'O.K., Bobby?'

'All set, sir,' Nye replied.

'I'll go in first, then,' Everitt said. 'Please stay outside to cover me.'

'Right, sir,' Nye answered. Dunstan Curtis waved in acknowledgement.

'Remember… a red flare, if you're to sugar off,' Everitt reminded them.

'Off we go.'

So the three M.G.B.s crept on silent engines round the eastern shore of the Île de Tatihou. As Wally sighted the black tower of the Fort de la Hougue standing gaunt against the low-lying coast, the clearing bearing of the fort on Tatihou slipped past on the binnacle card. Nye straightened himself from the bearing ring.

'Stop both. Get the landing craft alongside and embark pongos,' he murmured.

'Aye, aye, sir.' Number One raised his arm; then Wally heard the scrape of the L.C.P. as it was gently hauled alongside.

There was a muffled oath from the soldier who had slipped, and then the L.C.P.s disappeared into the darkness.

'We're right abeam of the whistle buoy,' Nye said. 'We'll recover them here.'

Wally felt his pulse quicken. The great Fort de la Hougue loomed blackly above them — surely the German gunners would spot them at any second?

'They *must* sight us soon,' Nye muttered, as he watched 316 intently. 'Wish the pongos would get a move on.'

'Blue light flashing "Q" ashore, sir,' the signalman said.

'Good, that's them. The Senior Officer's going in. Full ahead, Cox'n. Open fire on anything that pipes up, Number One.'

Wally could not see 316 or 314, but it was comforting to feel their presence as 312 hurtled into the jaws of the harbour. Tatihou castle was already coming abeam, and, as the gunboat roared up to full power to awaken the dead, a light blinked from the fortress battlements.

'Make the signal,' Nye shouted. 'It may buy us more time.' The Aldis clattered behind Wally's head:

*Permission to proceed in execution of previous orders…* the signal went out in Morse in German, the words memorised by the signalman.

Following his leader in 316, Bobby Nye in 312 charged inwards towards the group-occulting light on the outer extremity of the breakwater. White — then red — it occulted, regularly every six seconds, as Wally timed it by the sailors' mental clock:

*If I wasn't a gunner I wouldn't be here* — FIRE.' Five seconds precisely. *Yes,* thought Wally, *we're bang on target; just as well with these perishing rocks around.* He could see the white line of surf curling round the base of the rocks.

'Open fire!' Nye yelled as green and red tracer floated gracefully towards them from the Fort de l'Ilet. The boat shuddered as the Rolls gun replied, its 2-pounder shells exploding with pinpoints of orange flame on the masonry ashore. The coastal machine gun ceased abruptly. A cheer hailed from aft while the Rolls gunners searched for fresh targets. They had not long to wait.

A searchlight, blue-white in intensity, suddenly swept across the breakwater, while a heavier gun opened up across the bay from the Fort de la Hougue.

'Target, the searchlight,' Number One shouted to the Oerlikon on the fo'c's'le. 'Point of aim, the gun emplacement on the fort.'

The roar and clatter of the guns now shattered the night. Wally's eardrums ached from the sound, where he stood in the wings, the spare strip-Lewis to his shoulder as he lined up on a burst of small arms fire on the seaward end of the breakwater.

Nye was now calmly conning the boat, the throttles in his hands as the Cox'n at his feet below him spun the wheel.

'Nothing to starboard, Cox'n. There's a damn great rock close abeam. Steady on the breakwater light.'

'Aye, aye, sir.'

The gunboat was now streaking through the night, straight for the breakwater. Suddenly the searchlight beam swathed the boat in a dazzling white light.

'Put that blasted light out, can't you, Number One?' Nye called. 'Hard-a-port, Cox'n.' He flicked back the port throttle; the boat heeled crazily inwards as she twisted on her stern, her wake boiling and hissing where she turned. Wally heard a scream ashore, a shattering of glass, and the searchlight went out: he'd never felt so nude before and now came merciful oblivion as M.G.B. 312 was once more enfolded by the darkness.

Tracer was now curving and arcing across the little bay, less than half a mile wide. Somewhere ashore the Commandos must be, by now, capturing their prey. Nye was glowering at his watch.

'Steady, Cox'n. Steer one-five-o…'

The tracer was now criss-crossing in the mêlée, the gunboat staying up at the northern end of the bay while she fired on anything that moved.

'Green grenade, sir, from ashore,' the signalman shouted.

'Good. Pongos are shoving off,' Nye said. 'A few more minutes up here, Number One, and then we can get to hell out of it.'

'Bit noisy around here, sir,' the First Lieutenant muttered. 'You've spilt my ki, sir.'

'Here comes our L.C.P. Stand by to take her in tow, Number One,' Nye retorted. 'Keep a look out for 314's signal, Wally.'

'Aye, aye, sir.' Wally felt pleased that at last he had something useful to do. He still wasn't used to being shot at. Then suddenly, after an eternity of waiting, a red, then a green Verey's light floated into the night sky where the L.C.P. should have been recovered by Curtis in 314.

'Red and green Verey's light,' Wally shouted. 'Right astern of us, sir.'

'Good-o. Take our L.C.P. in tow and then we'll push off.'

The next two minutes were the longest in Wally's life so far. He would never forget the calm bearing of 312's captain as he stood on the bridge, arms folded, while he waited for their L.C.P. to bump alongside. The tow was passed and 31% slowly went ahead. The night was now a mass of flying shell and spiralling tracer, red, green and orange. The German defenders were busily engaging each other and most of the tracer was passing overhead.

'Full ahead together. Take her out on course one-eight-o, Cox'n.'

The boat took the strain of the tow then surged ahead and, as she steadied, Wally began to breathe again. But, as the whistle buoy came abeam, the whole boat juddered and shook as an explosion split wide the night above them.

The boat careered madly onwards, but above the racket Wally heard the groans of wounded men from the quarterdeck.

'Evans is hit, sir, and two are wounded,' Number One shouted. 'I'm going aft.'

Wally jumped towards the chart table to relieve his First Lieutenant. He wiped the cocoa from the chart and scanned the plan of the harbour.

'Course to clear the banks?' the Captain asked.

Wally ran the parallel ruler across the sodden chart. 'One hundred, sir.'

He felt the boat heel violently to port, heard the Captain shouting, and then they were clear — out and away, into the merciful mantle of the night.

'Blue light, sir, green four-o,' the starboard lookout reported calmly.

'Identification signal, sir,' the signalman called. *London-Apples.*'

'Very good. Steer o-nine-o, Cox'n.'

Formation was resumed on 316 as the tracer began falling astern while the battle raged ashore.

'Hope they continue for a long time yet,' Number One said as he climbed back to the bridge.

'Reminds me of the day an E-boat joined up in our line as tail-end Charlie. He'd got his knickers twisted,' Nye said. 'Stop both.'

312 sat down in the sea, her engines coughing and throbbing as she sidled towards the two dark outlines waiting for them. Everitt leant nonchalantly over his bridge rail. 'All right, Bobby?' he asked.

'One dead, two badly hurt, sir, I'm afraid.'

There was silence between the three boats where they wallowed in the sea less than a mile from Tatihou. There was nothing more to say.

'How many squareheads?' the Senior Officer continued.

'Four. They're dead.'

Everitt nodded. ''S'pose it was worth it.' He looked across at 314. 'How about you?'

'No casualties, sir,' Dunstan said. 'Easy as kiss your hand.' 316 increased speed as Nye moved forward his throttles. The engines growled again into a crescendo of sound. The boat leapt forward, while 314 slipped into station on the starboard beam.

'Course three-five-o, sir, for St Catherine's,' Wally said.

'Steer three-five-o, Cox'n,' the Captain ordered. 'Keep your eyes skinned. We've still got to slip through their patrols.'

# CHAPTER 8

### The Gubbins
### *Bruneval, 27th/28th February 1942*

On 11th February 1942, the German battle cruisers, *Scharnhorst* and *Gneisenau,* with the cruiser, *Prinz Eugen*, in company, made their dash up the Channel from Brest. In spite of relentless attacks by the Fleet Air Arm Swordfish torpedo bombers, under the leadership of Lieutenant-Commander Esmonde, D.S.O., who was posthumously awarded the Victoria Cross on behalf of those who flew with him; despite the heroic efforts of Lieutenant E. N. Pumphrey, D.S.O., D.S.C., and his M.T.B.s; in the face of a torpedo attack by the Harwich destroyers under Captain Pizey, D.S.O.; and in spite of a large-scale torpedo and bomber attack in atrocious weather off Holland by Bomber Command, the German naval force, though badly damaged, successfully reached its homeland.

Three weeks earlier, Wally Bruce had taken over command of M.G.B. 336, shortly after the St Vaast raid. For his First Lieutenant he had asked for Christopher Jannaway, who had joined Wally again after a spell in the Type IV Hunt destroyer, *Albrighton.* M.G.B. 336 had only just sufficient time to work up before being summoned at full speed to Ramsgate. The German battle cruiser's breakthrough took place the next day but the Ramsgate M.G.B.s took little part in the foray because of bad weather and timing. Wally then rejoined the Division of the Fourteenth M.G.B. Flotilla, which was still engaged on its role of small-scale raiding.

On the morning of 24th February 1942, Wally found himself in C-in-C's Operational Headquarters in Portsmouth Dockyard, assembled with the Commanding Officers of M.G.B.s 316 (Flotilla Leader, Lieutenant-Commander Everitt), 317 Coste, 312 Nye, 314 Curtis, who was soon to be detached for the St Nazaire raid; and, especially summoned from Great Yarmouth, M.G.B.s 315 (Mason) and 326 (Russell-Roberts). These men sat in a group together, a tight-knit bunch, while the other C.O.s, who were older men, tended to remain separate. Also present was the Captain of the large Landing Ship Infantry, H.M.S *Prince Albert*, who carried the 8th Landing Craft Assault Flotilla which consisted of six L.C.A.s and two L.C.S.s with Oerlikons.

The plan for the forthcoming operation was for a small force of Army paratroopers to be dropped by Whitleys upon Bruneval, a village twelve miles north-north-east of Le Havre. Outside the village, so Intelligence reported, was a German radio-location station, some four hundred yards away from the garrisoned farmhouse named 'Le Presbytère'. The R.A.F. Photographic Reconnaissance Units had also confirmed the presence of this enemy Radio Direction Finder station. If the apparatus could be captured and brought back to England, British scientists could discover how far, and with what accuracy, the enemy had progressed with RD/F, and therefore how Britain could counter the enemy's use of it. In addition, the examination of the 'Gubbins', as the apparatus came to be called, might reveal what risks the British bombers could be permitted to run when flying in to attack.

The soldiers, with the aid of a scientist specially trained for the operation, were to attack the radio location post, capture several German operators and give Priest, the scientist, time to cut out the Gubbins. Then, with prisoners and the Gubbins, the force was to return down the cliff, which would already have been secured by one section of the paratrooper force.

The L.C.A.s, having been carried over from Portsmouth by *Prince Albert,* would be lowered offshore; they would be towed to the landing beach by the M.G.B.s. On completion, the M.G.B.s would tow the L.C.A.s back to Portsmouth. M.G.B. 312's only function in this operation was to return safely at her best possible speed with the Gubbins and Priest.

Whilst this operation was in progress, Wally Bruce in M.G.B. 336 was to land two agents, undetected, some three miles northward of Bruneval. He was not told of his passengers' duties, but it was hinted that their mission was to prepare the French for an impending raid on the Normandy coast. The operation was to be thoroughly exercised at Arish Mell Gap in Worbarrow Bay, off Weymouth, where the shoreline and cliffs were remarkably similar to those off Bruneval. Wally was to proceed to Newhaven on the morning of 27th February.

At 1100 on 27th February 1942, Wally slipped M.G.B. 336 from H.M.S. *Hornet.* Passing through the Looe Channel, he increased to 25 knots and took his little ship four miles offshore along the Sussex coast: Littlehampton, with its Martello tower; Worthing Pier, with the unmistakable landmark of the woods of Chanctonbury Ring far away on the Downs; the power station chimneys of Shoreham, the excrescence of Brighton Pier, and then the easily identifiable cliff and long breakwater of Newhaven.

M.G.B. 336 secured on a catamaran alongside the jetty, abreast the railway station, so that Wally would not be worried by the large tidal range in Newhaven. Knowing that a long night lay ahead of them, he ordered his First Lieutenant to see that all hands got their heads down. Darkness came only too swiftly, and at 1800 all hands aboard M.G.B. 336 were fully awake, fresh, and itching to begin the operation, about which they knew nothing.

On the minute, as planned, two muffled figures materialised from the darkness behind the railway trucks. Wally watched Jannaway saluting the strangers as they slipped silently across the brow before being taken down to the ward room.

'Start up silent engines.'

The boat quivered as the engines fired: only the sound of the gentle coughing of the exhausts was audible now that the Dumbflo silencing devices were engaged. The Dumbflos were an essential requirement for successful Coastal Forces work.

'Slip.'

Wally turned her, inside her own length, then slipped silently down the centre of the harbour on the first of the ebb. It was pitch dark and few onlookers would have seen him slinking past the breakwater. Using the blue lantern, he 'made his pendants' with the Port War Signal Station in the hut high up on the cliff to the western side of the breakwater. An answering wink acknowledged his passing, and then he was past the breakwater light. He remained on silent engines until he was five miles south, then switched to main engines. The boat surged ahead, coming on to the plane as she lifted to her step. Wally felt his pulse quicken as his beautiful craft hitched up her skirts; with a breeze of Force 3 from the south west, a slight swell, and with the moon climbing from out of the eastern horizon, these were ideal conditions for cloak-and-dagger work.

'The whole object of Operation Biting is to avoid, rather than seek, opposition,' the Chief of Staff had said. 'And you, Bruce, in 336, must consider yourself as part of this operation.'

The briefing had been succinct, yet the operation had been planned to the last detail.

Wally dipped into his chart table to check his course. By the subdued blue lighting, he traced his pencilled course-line until it reached a point five miles off Cap d'Antifer, where he would make his landfall. If he was in luck, the d'Antifer light might be lit for a passing convoy. He could then nip unobserved round the stern of the convoy and coast-crawl southwards along the coast until he reached a point two miles north of the Bruneval party. If he was sighted, or brushed with the enemy, he was to cancel his part of the operation and return immediately to Newhaven.

He emerged from the chart table to find Jannaway standing by him.

'Take over, Number One. Course, one-eight-five.'

'Aye, aye, sir. Course one-eight-five.'

'What are our agents like?' Wally asked as he handed over the only pair of binoculars.

'Uncommunicative,' Number One replied. 'But where's the rest of Operation Biting, sir?'

'They left Pompey at 1715. *Prince Albert* is leading the force to F-buoy, where sweepers have cleared a lane across the minefield for her, so she can steer south to Bruneval.'

'*Bruneval?*'

'Yes, Bruneval. I'll tell you about the operation when I've seen the agents. Then I'd like to brief the ship's company.'

'Aye, aye, sir.'

Steadying himself from the bucking of the leaping boat, Wally eased himself below to the subdued light of the ward room, an 8-foot by 6-foot compartment on the starboard side of the ladder. He did not remove his duffle coat but only his cap. The two agents had taken off their outer garments, and in the gloom he could see that one was much smaller than the other, and a woman.

'Good evening,' he said. 'I hope you're being looked after.'

The man spoke up: 'Yes, thank you. We were given hot soup. *Magnifique…*'

'You're French, then?' Wally asked.

'Yes.'

Wally had the wit not to ask his name, but there was something in the crisp, precise tone of voice that seemed strangely familiar.

'And you, Madame,' Wally continued, addressing himself to the neat little figure. 'You are French, too?'

The woman nodded.

*They're not giving much away,* Wally thought. *They must be under fearful strain and obviously want to remain incognito.*

'Please let me know if there's anything we can do for you,' he said. 'You've got two hours before I put you ashore.'

*'Merci,'* said the man. 'You are *très gentil.'*

Wally turned to go, at a loss for words. He would never see this couple again once they were ashore. These agents needed a very special courage, a bravery of a different kind: alone, trusting no one, adrift in enemy territory… it must be hell.

Wally struggled on deck, where the rush of wind hit him in the face. He had a word with the gunners in their turrets before climbing below to talk to his men. Having put them all in the picture, the tension eased: this was another cloak-and-dagger party — nothing in it particularly, because 336, after landing these two spies, would be joining the Biting main force.

The passage across the Channel was uneventful. When five miles off Cap d'Antifer, Wally proceeded on silent engines. Though the d'Antifer light was not burning, he clearly identified the headland and, taking running fixes, obtained an accurate position.

'Half a mile to go, sir,' Jannaway reported from the chart table. He spoke quietly, barely audible above the gentle swish of the bow wave in this placid sea.

'Stand by the dinghy, Number One. Better get the agents on deck.'

Wally was crouching over his azimuth mirror. Two degrees to go before the headland came on the bearing.

'Port twenty, Cox'n. Steer one-one-o.'

The M.G.B. crept silently in towards the coast. Already Wally could see through his binoculars the thin white ribbon along the beach where the small breakers lazily curled. He hurriedly snapped the clearing bearings of Cap d'Antifer. Quarter of a mile to go and still undetected.

*'Monsieur le capitaine?'* a strained voice spoke in the darkness from the companionway at his feet. *'Merci, et bonne chance.'*

Wally turned towards the French agent who was edging past him, his aquiline features sharply outlined by the glow from the binnacle. Then recognition suddenly dawned on Wally. Of course, it was Gilbert Fragonard, the Chaser officer. Wally's previous dislike of the fellow evaporated with his respect for the Frenchman's courage.

'Good luck, *mon ami*,' Wally said.

From the darkness at the Frenchman's side there emerged the petite outline of his compatriot, the French girl. She came forward and touched Wally's sleeve.

'Please understand, *mon cher*,' the girl whispered, 'when they asked me to land with Gilbert, I had to do it.'

Wally stood motionless and silent for an instant, rigid with surprise. Then, his heart racing, he pressed Suzanne's hand.

'God keep you both,' he said as he gently turned her towards the upper deck where the dinghy party waited. 'Of course I understand.' He walked aft with them both, and handed her down into the dinghy which bobbed alongside.

The seaman bore off with the loom of his oar. Suzanne's pale oval face was peering up at him. 'I've asked them to see that you bring us back,' she murmured, her eyes shining as she waved.

'When?' Wally whispered. 'When, Sukie?'

But the dinghy was swallowed already in the darkness. From out of the night came the rhythmic splashes of the dinghy's oars… and then there was silence save for the surge of the breakers beneath the cliffs.

As Wally regained his bridge to turn 336 end-on to the shore, he caught the sound of aircraft engines growing louder at every second. The planes droned directly overhead to cross the cliffs a mile to the southward. The enemy guns started to fire, but some way inland. Perhaps, Wally hoped as he waited impatiently, the Whitleys were being mistaken by the enemy for a normal bombing raid?

He glanced at his watch. It was twenty minutes past midnight. The dinghy should have been back by now.

Bobby Nye would have been bored by this outward passage had it not been for the presence of Flight-Lieutenant Priest. This man was a brilliant scientist but was forced to wear R.A.F. uniform for this operation so that, if he were captured ashore, he could not, by international law, be shot as a spy.

Nye had, as with the others, taken his beloved M.G.B. 312 to exercise for this operation in Worbarrow Bay, between Lulworth and Weymouth. At last, here he was, escorting *Prince Albert* towards the dropping point less than a mile away. Bobby had carried out so many small-scale raids by now that he was becoming more confident with every month that passed; but he would never lose this hidden fear, this feeling of his innards turning to water, on each occasion before the moment of attack.

He watched the blinking blue light from Everitt in M.G.B. 316: *Prince Albert* was stopping now to lower her L.C.A.s.

'Stop both,' Nye ordered. He looked at his watch: 2152. Right on time. Now to take two L.C.A.s in tow. There they were, already sidling up towards him, with the black outlines of their skeleton crews huddled in the stern around the Cox'n's armoured wheelhouse.

'Stand by, Number One, to take 'em in tow.'

'Aye, aye, sir.'

Then, for the next two hours, the force plugged silently towards Cap d'Antifer. There were thirty-seven extra Army officers and men distributed amongst these little ships whose task it was to cover the withdrawal of the paratroopers when they brought back the Gubbins.

At 2345, Everitt, with the Naval Force Commander, Commander F. N. Cook, R.A.N. aboard, reduced speed still further and switched to silent engines. The L.C.A.s were then slipped. Bobby then shook hands with Priest who, axe in hand and escorted by four Commando brigands, clambered into the L.C.A. which had hauled up alongside. Then, as the L.C.A.s shoved off into the darkness, Bobby heard the sound of aircraft droning overhead. Seconds later he saw the flak some way inland.

The worst part of the operation was now to follow: the anxious period of waiting before being summoned inshore to re-embark the troops. Bobby ran the palm of his hand over his gas-operated Vickers gun: he would occasionally, when very frightened, loose off a few rounds for Dutch courage. He smiled as he glanced at his wristwatch in the darkness. It was twenty minutes past midnight.

Major J. D. Frost of the First Airborne Division had briefed his men for the last time: his six officers and 113 men were trained to the highest pitch of efficiency and morale. If any raid were to succeed, this one should. He felt a surge of pride as he watched his men, in their rubber-edged paratroopers' helmets and rubber-soled boots, board, cat-like, the Whitleys which, engines already roaring, were waiting on the tarmac. Frost felt confident: in the leading aircraft was Wing Commander Pickard, D.S.O. and Bar, D.F.C., a splendid and reliable commander. The door of the Whitley slammed shut behind him, the aircraft shuddered to the extra surge of power and they were off.

Frost glanced through the pilot's window. Conditions were perfect tonight: no wind, a bright moon with a little cloud, a slight haze. He grinned as he listened to his men singing with gusto 'Annie Laurie', 'Lulu', and the paratroopers' song, 'Come sit by my side if you love me'.

Flight Sergeant E. W. F. Cox was singing solo, 'The Rose of Tralee', in a raucous baritone. He was a skilled radio engineer and had volunteered to dismantle the RD/F set when he made his rendezvous with Flight-Lieutenant Priest. Cox had learnt to jump in three weeks, which was no mean feat. Amongst these skilled men were distributed the only other 'foreigners': nine sappers and four signallers, for detonation and communications purposes.

It was not long before the Whitleys crossed the French coast and were approaching the dropping zone.

*'Prepare to jump.'*

Frost stood up. His men joined him silently by the door as they snapped their parachute lines to the jump wire. The warning light glowed in the darkness. The cold air blasted into the fuselage of the aircraft as the door was slammed open.

The red light flashed on.

*'Jump!'*

Except for two Whitleys, in one of which was Lieutenant E. C. B. Charteris, the jump was perfect, the drop pinpointing the target area; the only error was these two Whitleys which were a few minutes late, having been forced off course by a dose of flak.

They all knew that timing was vital to the success of the operation and to their chances of returning to England. Frost and his party had successfully attacked and captured the isolated house near the RD/F post. Flight Sergeant Cox and his sappers had also succeeded in dismantling the apparatus so that Priest, with whom they had made a successful rendezvous, could chop out the vital cathode-ray tube. This had taken time and, as they struggled frantically to free the Gubbins, part of the machinery which Cox held in his hands was struck by two bullets. Priest's axe swung frenziedly and then they were away, led by Major Frost and Lieutenant Vernon with his platoon, down towards the beach.

To their dismay they were met by a hail of fire. Charteris had not yet arrived to capture and hold the beach off, which they were to re-embark into the L.C.A.s which the Navy would be sending in shortly.

Frost groaned. The timing was going haywire: unless they could secure the beach, there'd be no hope of regaining the L.C.A.s. The tide was already ebbing and the Germans were reacting swiftly by sending in reinforcements behind him. What the devil had happened to Charteris?

As the silk and rigging lines of Lieutenant Charteris's parachute fell softly around him, he felt a pang of dismay and fear: having anxiously glanced around to gain his bearings, he could not identify, according to the briefing, the row of trees at the bottom of the valley; nor did the valley seem deep enough. Already his men were closing in on him, seeking orders. He groaned inwardly; he was lost, dropped in the wrong valley.

Then, close overhead, two Whitleys lumbered northwards, trundling back towards the sea. Thank God for this clue to his whereabouts; he must be too far inland. He started off at the paratrooper's rapid lope, halfway between a walk and a trot, crouched double, weapons at the ready.

He led his men across the slope of the valley and due northwards until, mercifully, he glimpsed through the bare trees the moonlight reflecting from the white lighthouse of Cap d'Antifer. At last he knew where he was.

He had begun crossing the ravine near Bruneval when his contingent stumbled into a straggling platoon of Germans. In the confusion, one German in the shadows joined up with Charteris's men; a mistake was made by the paratroopers, who did not notice for some while that they had an extra man at the end of the line. Awareness of the position was simultaneous — and fatal to the German, who was killed instantly.

They reached the crest of the ravine and were immediately halted by concentrated shooting from the outskirts of Bruneval. A murderous fire stemmed from a house on the beach, close to the right of the village. Charteris gathered his men, then stealthily fanned out to attack. In the shadows he almost collided with Major Frost, his Commanding Officer.

'Thank God you're here,' Frost said. 'I'm being held up; can't get down to the beach, and we're running out of time.'

'I wouldn't enjoy spending the rest of the war here,' said Charteris. 'I'll rush the cove while you hold them here, sir.'

Frost nodded. Charteris passed the word to his men, then raised his arm.

'*Charge!*' he yelled. He lowered his arm, then began running towards the house. which was now some seventy yards away. Although Charteris heard his comrades shouting and yelling on both sides of him, he felt as naked as a baby as he led the desperate charge. Dipping, weaving and sprinting, faster than he had ever known, he was surprised to find he was still alive when within twenty yards of the house. He swung his arm, and the first grenade lobbed through an open window on the ground floor.

After suffering similar treatment from the rest of his squad, the house crackled into flames. The squealing Germans were cut down as they bolted, while others of his platoon silenced the neighbouring pillbox, which, with its machine guns, was enfilading the beach. Not a Hun was spared. The beach was now safe.

In a room of the house on the beach, a German telephone orderly was in the act of telephoning his superior in Le Havre. He was still holding the receiver in his hand when a fresh shower of grenades rained upon the house.

'I can't hear you,' said a weary guttural voice from Le Havre.

'*Mein Leutnant...*' the orderly was shouting down the mouthpiece as Charteris burst into the room, revolver drawn.

'Speak up, can't you?' the officer in distant Le Havre was shouting. 'There's a devil of a noise in the background.'

The orderly dropped the instrument back to its rest and raised his hands in surrender.

'Come on, Fritz,' Charteris said, motioning the man towards the beach. 'You're coming back to England with us.'

The raiders then hid themselves at the foot of the cliffs, while Major Frost flashed to seaward with his blue torch. The tide line was already receding, and the enemy was breathing down their necks and shooting from above. This wait was agonising.

Frost glanced at his watch. The time was half past two in the morning and there was still no sign of the Navy.

Able Seaman Herbert Rand, Trained Man, Royal Navy, was port lookout in M.G.B. 317. He stamped his feet and blew on his mittened hands as the M.G.B. waited to take in the L.C.A.s for the second time in order to bring off the pongos.

'Lookouts, keep your eyes skinned to seaward,' the Captain ordered quietly. Bert Rand had joined M.G.B. 317 at Gosport and, as soon as he was aboard, he knew that he had joined a happy ship. An Able Seaman, Trained Man, was the general dogsbody on any ship, but was certainly one of the vertebrae of a small ship. Rand had liked Coste as soon as he'd set eyes on him: an intelligent, quiet and thoughtful Captain.

*Funny,* Rand thought, *how different the shoreline looks from the cliffs of Worbarrow Bay where we exercised this operation: probably snow on the cliff top. Normally a cliff top is darker than the cliffs and the skyline, but this effect is weird... looks wrong...*

Anyway, judging by the shooting ashore, the pongos must be getting on with the job, but he'd be glad when it was over. Trust Bert Rand to step right up to his neck in it, on his first trip in his first M.G.B. Bit different to a life in a battle wagon...

M.G.B. 317 lay at anchor to her rope warp: the hawser could be cut and noiselessly dropped over the side, in case a quick and silent getaway was needed. If the enemy stumbled upon the raiding force, it was 317's role to lead the naval force out of the area.

'Keep your eyes skinned!'

It was the Old Man again: must be edgy tonight — but the Captain had a sixth sense, they said. *It's cold*, Rand thought, *damned cold*.

He concentrated again on his lookout sector. Time was dragging and the moon was now well into the night sky. Any enemy down-moon of them could easily creep up unobserved. 'Come on,' Herbert Rand muttered to himself. 'Wake up. Everyone aboard this hooker depends on your perishin' eyes.'

Backwards and forwards across the horizon line he searched, as he'd been taught so often. The darkness seemed denser there. He swung his eyes back again: yes, a darker smudge. His heart hammered — two smudges to seaward of them, and closing rapidly.

'Captain, sir,' he reported tersely, 'two unidentified ships, green three-o.'

Coste picked up the enemy immediately. He hailed quietly across to Everitt, his S.O. in 316.

'O.K., John,' came the reply. 'I've spotted 'em.'

'Stand by to cut the cable,' Coste ordered. 'Target, two small destroyers.'

It was comforting to hear the whirr of the power-operated turrets as the 0.5s came on.

'Two E-boats, sir, on either bow of the destroyers,' Rand reported.

'Very good.'

Coste had the situation in hand. Rand watched his captain's gauntleted hand as it hung poised upon the alarm push. If that was pressed, the engines would roar into life, the cable would be cut, and then out to attack the enemy — but then the soldiers ashore would have to be abandoned and left to their fate.

'Stand by,' Coste murmured.

The dark silhouettes were huge now... They were sliding rapidly past, less than six hundred yards away, gigantic, they were so close.

Rand held his breath. The enemy were creeping silently, deliberately down-moon of them so that they could line up the M.G.B.s in their gun sights, up-moon. It was the perfect attacking position, with your target against the golden and shimmering path of the moon; while you could see him clearly, he could not see you.

Rand swallowed hard. What a way to end his first patrol in M.G.B.s! His hands were shaking as he watched Coste, motionless and tense, surveying the darkened ships like a lynx.

The trained man could feel the thumping of his heartbeat in his ears... all was so still, just the lapping of the tide against the boat's hull; the hiss of the water as the enemy ships slid silently past.

Then the destroyers turned abruptly to port, towards Le Havre; they merged into the night, invisible, vanishing as swiftly as they had materialised.

'Thank God for our Plymouth Pink,' the Captain muttered. 'That saved us this time, against the cliffs.'

Rand sighed. Yes, thank God... this pink paint must have merged into the shoreline, or they certainly would have been sighted. The whole operation had depended upon the alertness of men's eyes.

'A near one, Number One,' Coste said. 'I bet Bobby Nye had the wind up. If the shooting had started, he'd never have got back with the Gubbins.'

Twenty minutes later, the M.G.B.s weighed anchor and escorted the L.C.A.s into the beach. Firing became intense from the cliff top, an engagement ensuing whilst the L.C.A.s waited for the last of the rearguard to embark. This caused delay, and because the L.C.A.s had not appeared at the scheduled time, Everitt took his M.G.B.s into the beach to hasten events.

Recognition signals were hurriedly exchanged, and then the Gubbins was humped aboard Bobby Nye's boat. Then, as the wounded and their prisoners were being embarked, 312's engines roared into life. A white cascade showed at her stern, and Bobby Nye was off like a bat out of hell.

The fire was now becoming intense from the cliff top. As the L.C.A.s were finally compelled to shove off, the paratroopers on board watched the fire from seven of their comrades, who had become separated, gradually dying away as they were overwhelmed. The naval force then disappeared, whence it had sprung, into the darkness of the Channel.

Able Seaman Rand first knew that this was a paratroopers' raid when he hauled the first soldier on board: the man, a sergeant, was wearing an egg-shaped helmet surrounded by spongy rubber. He was chattering with cold, having swum out a hundred yards from the beach so as not to be left behind.

'Cor — I'm frozen, Jack,' the man spluttered between chattering teeth. 'Where's the engine room, so I can get warm?'

317 was now under way and shepherding the L.C.A.s into shape, so that they could be towed home. Rand helped the sergeant down into the engine room, where hoar frost glinted

on top of the cooling manifolds and where the stokers were clad in duffle coats.

''Struth!' the soldier said. 'What is this? A seaborne fridge?'

'All right, matey,' Rand said. 'Come on to the mess deck. It's warm there and we've got some rum.'

The seamen's mess deck was only thirteen feet square and was crammed with soldiers. Hot soup and cocoa were bubbling away on the galley stove, but already the wind was getting up. The M.G.B. began wallowing across the quartering sea, and by three o'clock the wind had freshened to Force 5.

The soldier-passengers and all hands off-watch were spread around the mess deck and were snatching a few minutes' sleep. The large canteen of cocoa and the 'fanny' of soup slid across the galley stove, where they came up all-standing against the 'fiddles' to tip over and fall off the paraffin stove which was extinguished by the utensils as they fell. In falling, the 'fanny' knocked the plunger knob of the fire extinguisher. In a few seconds the corticene on the deck, upon which were stretched the exhausted sleepers, was smothered in cocoa, soup, foam from the extinguisher, and paraffin. The paraffin fumes from the extinguished stove were soon to ensure that anyone who was not already sick would soon join the rest. In this wind and sea the force was making only six and a half knots. As the first rays of dawn streaked the eastern horizon, silver and pastel green, the raiders were still only fifteen miles from the French coast.

Bert Rand had retired to the upper deck to snatch sleep. He crouched behind the 0.5-inch turret when, from out of the northern twilight, the welcome drone of R.A.F. Spitfires began slowly to drown the silence of the passage homewards. Then appeared four French Chasers, barely visible in their Plymouth Pink. Spread out on either bow loomed the larger shapes of two Hunts, *Blencathra* and *Fernie*, who had been despatched to escort the force home.

Thus, at 1630 on 28th February 1942, the naval force for Operation Biting returned to Spithead. For the loss of six killed, five wounded, and six left behind and missing, the vital Gubbins had, with Bobby Nye, safely reached England at 1000. Prisoners had been taken, but most valuable of all, terror had been struck into the hearts of the enemy, so that the Germans were compelled to reinforce their Normandy coastline with more troops.

Bobby Nye had every reason to feel proud when, on return, he read his personal signal from Commander F. N. Cook, Royal Australian Navy, Commanding Officer of the Naval Force and of H.M.S. *Tormentor,* the base in the Hamble:

*Please accept yourself and convey to all Commanding Officers and men under your command my sincere gratitude for your willing and efficient co-operation on this recent party which could not have taken place without you. I am sorry that, for security reasons, you are not getting the publicity you have earned. It has been a real pleasure to have worked with the boats.*

Bobby Nye grinned as he slapped the stock of his G.O. Vickers gun.

'To hell with publicity,' he muttered. 'Let's get on with the next raid.' As he looked up at *Hornet* from his bridge in the trots, he saw 336 come limping in on one engine, an hour adrift. 'Hullo, Wally. Lost your way, chum?'

Bruce was unsmiling as he pointed to his port quarter.

'Hit something as I came astern from the beach,' he said mournfully. 'I've damaged an A-bracket, I'm sure; water's coming in aft.'

Nye grimaced. 'Bad luck, Wally. Hurry up and put it right. As soon as we're stored and ammunitioned we're off again.' Grinning hugely, he began to whistle 'It's a long way to go home'.

As soon as 336 had bumped alongside, Wally Bruce hurled his cap at his Senior Officer.

# CHAPTER 9

*The Sleuth: Motor Torpedo Boats*
*1941/42*

The damage to M.G.B. 336's 'A' bracket was extensive: frames had fractured, the shaft had bent, and the bolts had twisted through the boat's bottom planking. She would be in dockyard hands for at least a month.

Wally Bruce was in the depths of depression when Nye approached him in *Hornet*'s ward room. 'All right for some,' he said, clapping Wally on the back. 'Some people are privileged.'

'Why?' Wally asked, not amused.

'I'm spending all my time on this small-scale raiding force, but you've been appointed to Peter Dickens's boat. He's Senior Officer of the Twenty-first M.T.B. Flotilla. Cheer up, old son.'

Wally needed encouragement. He'd run into Paul Boyle, First Lieutenant and Staff Officer of the Chaser Base, who had told him that news of Fragonard and Suzanne had been received through an intercepted VHF transmission from the French Resistance. Apparently they were both one jump ahead of the Germans and hoped to be taken off according to plan, but in spite of delicate probing at Cowes, Wally had discovered nothing more. She might be dead by now, shot against a wall or caught one dark night by the Gestapo. He felt sick inside.

But this was no good. He'd have to forget, and pray that she'd come through... at least Fragonard was resourceful, and he did care for her. Wally pulled himself together, packed his bags and walked across the trot to *Hornet to* find his new Senior Officer.

'I'm glad you've come,' said Dickens. 'I'm short-handed at the moment and you'll gain experience while your boat's being patched up. Better report to Fison in 237. I'm going in his boat tonight.'

Lieutenant Peter Dickens, M.B.E., Royal Navy, great-grandson of Charles Dickens, was twenty-five years of age. He was stockily built and of a reserved nature. His dark hair and gingerish beard, which were always neatly trimmed, framed an oval face whose pallor betrayed long nights of strain and sleeplessness. The level gaze of his hazel-brown eyes missed nothing. He was the epitome of the professional naval officer, a serious, thoughtful man, trained to lead.

Two years ago he had been First Lieutenant of the Hunt-class destroyer, H.M.S. *Cotswold* when she had been caught by mines laid overnight by a marauding foray of E-boats. With her back broken and with a centre-line 40-foot hole running for'd from 'A' boiler room, she had stayed afloat only because of the flat calm.

Lieutenant-Commander Robert Peverell Hichens had roared out with his Sixth M.G.B. Flotilla from H.M.S. *Beehive* off Aldeburgh and had taken off *Cotswold*'s casualties. This was to be the first time that Peter met 'Hitch': the professional exponent of M.T.B. warfare meeting the outstanding leader of the M.G.B.s. These two men were destined to transform this ruthless warfare from that of bald-headed gallantry into one of skilled professionalism. Together they were to fight relentlessly their opponents in the E-boats and German destroyers, until Hitch was killed by a stray explosive shell when returning from patrols in 1943. He was then thirty-four. He has remained a legendary figure ever since.

The road, however, was uphill and long: with inadequate armament and apathy in bureaucratic quarters, the M.T.B.s and M.G.B.s had to prove themselves before the men at the top would take the 'Costly Farces' (as the Coastal Forces were nicknamed) seriously. The flotillas were not yet properly organised, the boats were unreliable, and no real thought had been given to tactics. Peter Dickens was, however, quick to learn by his mistakes. He had been learning for some time now.

The spare officer, Sub-Lieutenant D. G. Gill, R.N.V.R., had barely settled Wally into his new ward room when Dickens took his Twenty-first Flotilla to sea on its first serious action. The flotilla consisted of seventy-foot Vosper boats, powered by three American Packards, and capable of 40 knots. The drive for the two wing engines was conventional, but the centre propeller shaft was driven through a V-drive. Later, because of their poor turning circles, these boats were fitted with three rudders.

Though initially supplied with Mark V torpedoes, these were soon replaced by 21-inch Mark VIIIs, torpedoes identical with those fired by submarines. The Mark Vs were unreliable and seldom ran straight, two even crossing each other on several occasions. It was humiliating sometimes, having achieved a perfect firing position, for the 'fish' to run wild or deep. Dickens liked to approach to five hundred yards before firing and from sixty degrees on the bow.

There were only three boats fit for sea: Fison in 237, Macdonald, the youngest C.O. in M.T.B.s, in 241, and Ian Trelawny in 232. Dickens had his 'Yeoman' with him, Ordinary Seaman Haines — an excellent man — and he felt better. They cast off on time and slipped down Haslar Creek.

They were soon past Fort Blockhouse, into Spithead and through the boom to the open sea.

They were now 'on the step' and planing at 25 knots. It was cold, wet and miserable, but soon they'd be off Barfleur. Wally glanced aft: the boats were in their usual arrowhead formation, each boat being stationed only twenty feet from the next ahead, and tearing along just in front of her wake. The C.O.s had practised station-keeping until they were sick of it: quarterline gave instant communication by shouting and provided the best chance of surprise. As soon as the enemy was sighted they would stop, with engines cut for the sake of silence, to formulate their plans. When the details had been repeated by shouting back across the water, the boats would move in for the attack.

They had closed up at Action Stations and Barfleur could not be far off now: the seas were becoming confused near the race, and there was a strong tide running. Wally thought of Bobby Nye and their attack on St Vaast: a different life in gunboats. He wondered, from his position at the mast step, how Bobby was enjoying working with Appleyard, that magnificent Commando leader who was shortly to lead the raid on the Casquets Lighthouse when the German garrison was somewhat embarrassed at breakfast. Bobby Nye's sole existence seemed now to be concerned with small-scale raiding at the request of Captain 'Jock' Hughes-Hallett, R.N., who was now commanding Combined Operations Headquarters in Cowes.

When they were six miles off Cap Barfleur, Dickens altered course to the south-east to comb the enemy's convoy route. Shortly afterwards they reduced to auxiliary engines. Then, from the darkness, Dickens heard Macdonald in 241 singing out that he'd sighted the enemy. Dickens passed his orders, then started main engines. With a roar the M.T.B.s swung into the attack.

'Ah, now I can see 'em,' Dickens muttered to himself. 'There's a large screen and several merchant ships.' He leant across and shouted to his Commanding Officers:

'Mac, you take the van; Ian, take the big chap in the rear. I'll attack in the centre. We'll go straight in. All set?'

'Aye, aye, sir.'

'All set, sir.'

Three minutes had elapsed before Dickens moved ahead towards the enemy convoy, which was steering up-channel and close inshore to the rocky coast east of Barfleur.

'Stand by to fire torpedoes.' Dickens eased his throttles, M.T.B. 237 slowly losing way — torpedoes could only be fired at about 12 knots or they would plunge straight into the sea bed — but the M.T.B. was forced first to penetrate the enemy screen.

'They've got the big boys out tonight, Cox'n. Can you see that trawler?' The dark outline of a large armed trawler, less than a quarter of a mile away, was sliding slowly past them.

'Yes, sir.'

'Steer to pass close astern of her. We'll slip through there.'

'Aye, aye, sir.'

Then, suddenly, all hell was let loose as the enemy opened up with all he had.

'Damn, they've sighted us first,' Dickens cursed. 'Full ahead. I'm going straight in.'

There was the agonising wait for twenty seconds whilst the main engines were clutched in, and then the engines burst into life and 237 roared towards the alerted enemy. Wally eased towards the protection of the armoured bridge as the night suddenly became as day. Tracer criss-crossed blindingly as the three M.T.B.s dispersed towards their targets. Wally felt naked as the firing lit up the bridge, throwing everything into dark shadows and bold relief. Blinding tracer was now streaming towards them and cannon shells were exploding into the sea to ricochet, whining into the night.

237's 0.5-inch guns were blazing away as, now flat out, she dashed blindly towards the foe, desperately searching for her prey.

'I can't see a thing,' Dickens yelled. 'For God's sake, keep a good lookout.'

The enemy shells were now finding their mark. 237 was shuddering from repeated blows, but miraculously no one was as yet hit by the flying metal.

'Steering's gone, sir,' the Cox'n shouted. He looked upwards at his captain, Fison, and there was anxiety in his eyes.

To the westward, Trelawny had also been struck. His steering had gone too, his rudder to starboard, so that he turned short, unable to reach his firing position. His engine room had been hit and his crew were out of action with carbon monoxide poisoning. He was desperately trying to gain bearing at 12 knots on his target, a merchant ship. Then he found himself near the rocks, with enemy guns ashore also joining in the battle.

Then Peter Dickens in 237 suddenly saw a large ship ahead of him.

'Stand by!' he yelled, his head along the torpedo sight as he set his deflection. His rudder was jammed amidships, but he might as well loose off his fish. 'Get a gentle swing on to port, Cox'n.'

'Aye, aye, sir.'

'Two or three degrees to go ... *Stand by!*'

'*Stand by!*' the Cox'n shouted back.

'That's right … gently … FIRE!'

Dickens squeezed the torpedo triggers. The torpedomen struck the firing-pins with their wooden mallets in case the firing mechanism failed to act.

*'Full ahead!'*

'There's only one chance,' Dickens shouted. 'I'm going straight through the convoy and out the other side.'

237 knew she was in mortal danger. She picked up her skirts and flashed through the blinding cauldron. Tracer, starshell, smoke … all hell seemed to be let loose, and the M.T.B.s were suffering terrible punishment.

Wally had known fear before, but never like this. It was all very well to stand up and fight in a gunboat, but in an M.T.B. there was little with which to hit back.

A series of juddering blows struck the boat and Wally felt the heat of flames from below. 'God, this is it,' he whispered to himself as 237, completely out of control, swept under the gigantic counter of a merchant ship's stern less than thirty yards away.

'Get that fire under control, Number One,' Fison shouted. 'Tell the engine room to get up top.'

237 was now clear of the enemy, who had stopped firing. A searchlight from Cap Barfleur caught the doomed M.T.B. but the light was extinguished as soon as the Oerlikon opened fire on it. 237 was burning from end to end, but was not settling.

*My God!* Peter Dickens thought in utter dejection. *What a way to lead my flotilla. Sunk and lost on my first patrol. God forgive me… I must abandon ship. There's no need for this relentless slaughter.*

As he was about to order 'Stand by the rafts,' the familiar shape of Macdonald's M.T.B. 241 loomed from out of the smoke.

'Want a tow, Peter?' he shouted.

'I'm past that, I'm afraid, Mac. Take us off, will you?'

Macdonald calmly manoeuvred his boat alongside 237. No one had seen him, and miraculously he had not yet been hit. Whilst Fison and Dickens destroyed the confidential books, the wounded and the dead were swiftly transferred across to the M.T.B. wallowing alongside. As Macdonald went astern to draw clear, Wally watched 237 slowly burn herself out. It was over half an hour before she slipped beneath the waves and was gone.

Macdonald opened up his engines and they were away, flat out and steering northwards to wait for Trelawny. Twenty minutes later Trelawny, unsure of 241's identification, kept well clear to limp pitifully homewards independently. The two boats wallowed slowly back across the Channel, their crews feeling whipped, dejected, outwitted. Peter Dickens remained silent, his spirit never before so low in his life.

'By God,' he whispered to himself, 'never again; never, never again will I attack like that. From now on I'll use my brains.'

From that night on, Dickens grew in stature as the leading exponent of M.T.B. warfare. He'd taken a licking, and the Hun had won – but not for long.


From the time of the abortive attack off Barfleur, Dickens would informally assemble all his C.O.s after each operation. In the ward room, over a gin, the attack of the previous night would be analysed. Using matchsticks to represent their own craft and those of the enemy, the battle would be re-enacted countless times until finally a pattern began to emerge. It soon became evident to Peter that this was a cat-and-mouse game, and that his opponents were as full of guile and skill as was his own gallant band. Every new move was counterchecked, each new tactic was challenged in subsequent events. The enemy was even stopping sometimes, to confuse the calculations of the M.T.B. captains.

It took many operations and much tragic experience to find the right answer, but it was the professional and analytic approach of Peter Dickens which forged the tactics that enabled British coastal forces to regain the initiative. Not for nothing did Dickens earn the affectionate nickname of 'The Sleuth'.

One such link in the chain took place shortly after the Barfleur defeat. Peter had now convinced his C.O.s of the merits of the silent approach, and he trained them to a high pitch of efficiency in his new tactics. The C.O.s were learning all the time — most of all Wally Bruce, who was now attached to 234 as spare officer. He was beginning to understand the guile and the cold courage required of the M.T.B. man.

Peter Dickens was happiest when leading his flotilla in his own boat, M.T.B. 234. On one moonlight night, however, when operating from *Beehive* at Felixstowe, he was leading his flotilla in 224 off the Dutch coast when he sighted two trawlers. He left half his force to seaward, with orders to attack once he had reached a position inshore where he would create a diversion.

Taking the other half of his force with him, Dickens crept around the enemy until he was inshore of the trawlers. Then he sighted the fat outline of a small merchant ship silhouetted against the sparkling path of the moon. He decided to attack this target himself.

The visibility had decreased, and Peter had now managed to creep in to 500 yards. The enemy must have been keeping a lookout to seaward only: Peter lined up his torpedo sight. He crouched over the bar and waited for his sights to come on.

This was too easy: he had set no deflection, and he would fire only one torpedo to save those expensive weapons.

'Ready starboard.'

'Starboard tube ready, sir,' the seaman torpedoman reported quietly.

'Stand by.' Peter squinted along the sighting bar. Still no reaction from the enemy. 'Let her swing gently, Cox'n, very gently.'

'Aye, aye, sir.'

The graticule crept slowly up the side of the target, past the quarter, creeping imperceptibly past the funnel until it crossed the bridge.

*'Fire starboard!'*

Wally felt the tension as the command rang from the bridge. He waited for the slight shudder as the 'fish' slipped over the side... but nothing happened, nothing but a ghastly silence. Then Dickens's voice shouted angrily to the seaman on the tube:

'Why the devil haven't you hit it with your mallet, you ruddy fool?'

'Sorry, sir — lost me mallet.'

234 had now swung off target, and Peter Dickens's anger flared uncontrollably as he lashed the seaman with his tongue.

''Ere we are, sir,' the man said suddenly as he found his mallet.

'Don't fire!' yelled Dickens urgently, the boat's swing having continued and taken the sight past the target.

'Fire, sir?' acknowledged the seaman torpedoman. He struck the firing-pin a shrewd blow.

Dickens could control himself no longer. He left the bridge and stamped aft along the deck to the offending seaman.

'What the hell d'you think you're doing, you giddy idiot? I've never seen such incompetence in all my life. Good grief, man, can't you see you've chucked a two-thousand-pound fish away?'

'Sorry, sir. I didn't...'

Dickens rounded on 224's captain.

'Dammit, man, it's about time you trained your ship's company properly. Stop all leave until you've drilled everyone efficiently. I want your reasons in writing.'

There was a long silence of discomfiture. Then suddenly the night exploded into a gigantic firework display: the target had disintegrated in a sheet of flame, with leaping debris in every direction, which left trails of sparks and tracer in the night sky. Not a soul on board could have known what had hit them.

'I think you've hit, sir,' said 224's captain quietly.

Dickens felt the tension deflate like a balloon. He began roaring with laughter at his own mistake.

'She was a little ammo ship by the look of her. I would have missed by miles on my original sighting...' He walked back to the bridge, chuckling to himself. 'Full ahead,' he ordered. 'Let's get out of here.'

*What a man,* Wally thought. No wonder his troops respected him.

The Sleuth soon built up the Twenty-first Flotilla's efficiency. Then, one forenoon, a report from the R.A.F. indicated that an enemy convoy was coast-hopping up-Channel by night, from the Channel Islands to Cherbourg, to Le Havre, on to Boulogne and so up to The Hook, off the Dutch coast.

During the lunchtime session Peter Dickens summoned his C.O.s, and with his matchsticks they planned the night's impending operations. Tonight there would be four boats out of a possible seven; those left behind were either in maintenance or broken down. There would be four gunboats as escorts and to create diversions.

After lunch all the crews would get their heads down, while the ordnance artificers and the Wrens made their final checks on the guns. The Wrens were marvellous workers: they took an intense pride in their own respective guns and their individual gunners. After each patrol, and after each firing, these complicated automatic guns, the 0.5-inch Vickers on their Boulton-Paul mountings, would have to be unshipped and wiped down, while the job of belting up ammunition continued interminably.

'Did my gun work all right?' the Wrens would ask. 'How'd you get on?' There was a wonderful feeling of hero-worship between these young women and their men behind the guns.

Then, promptly at 1600, after a final briefing, Peter Dickens and his officers trooped down to the boats, muffled to the eyebrows in warm clothing and with a minimum of uniform. Peter was reaching the end of the jetty when he heard footsteps running after him. He turned to see Petty Officer Douglas Ross saluting him.

'What d'you want?' Dickens asked.

'May I come to sea with you, sir?' the man said breathlessly. 'My boat is unserviceable.'

'Why? What's the point?'

'Got me own gun, sir.'

Peter smiled — at least the chap was keen.

'An old Strip-Lewis, sir.'

The Senior Officer paused a moment to consider.

'All right, provided I don't have to wait for you.'

Petty Officer Ross saluted, then rushed back along the jetty to collect his gun. The peace of the base was then shattered by the roar of engines as the Senior Officer led his flotilla out of the harbour. With the hands fallen in on the fo'c's'le and abreast the tubes, they sprang to attention as the bo'sun's calls shrilled. The Captain of the Base would always be standing there, taking the salute as his boats slid past him, their battle ensigns fluttering proudly from their miniature gaffs.

Having set course for the corner of Holland off Terschelling, Dickens settled down in the charthouse for a sleep, while Wally took over as watch-keeper. With the sun setting behind him and with the dew falling, it was damp and cold — and yet the chill in the pit of his stomach, the fear that was always with one, had nothing to do with the cold of the winter's night.

The flotilla had over 140 miles to go, to the limit of their endurance; this meant a five-and-a-half-hour passage there and back at 25 knots. When they were halfway across, a blue lamp began winking astern.

'Another breakdown, sir,' Wally reported. 'She's losing oil pressure.'

Dickens was immediately awake and cursing at Wally's side. 'Stop,' he ordered, racking his brains whether to send this last boat home also (he had already sent two back) or waste time trying to repair the breakdown.

As the boat sat down in the water, the M.G.B.s immediately conformed.

'Have you tried the V-drive oil pressure?' Dickens shouted across to the broken-down boat.

The waiting was infuriating. Dickens grew more impatient as the minutes passed: this was to be his second combined attack with the gunboats. If the co-operation with the M.G.B.s this time was going to be as good as it was with Leaf's boats, when he and Peter had accounted for one supply ship, all augured well for tonight. The M.G.B.s were keeping good station to starboard: he could see their silhouettes where they wallowed, waiting, waiting impatiently to forge on to Holland.

Then Dickens heard the reply across the water: 'O.K. How did you guess?'

The force of M.T.B.s and M.G.B.s set off again, a vital twelve minutes lost; but this decision was always an agonising one for the Senior Officer to make.

When twelve miles off Terschelling, Dickens luckily ran across an enemy buoy he had used before. This fixed his position, so he maintained his speed to catch up his suspected convoy. He would have to accept the noise: the gunboats would have to compensate for loss of surprise by attracting the enemy's attention when contact was made. His force was in arrowhead formation, the M.T.B.s to port, the gunboats to starboard.

'Action Stations,' he ordered. An enemy radio report had been received, confirming that a convoy was ahead of them on a north-easterly course as it sneaked along the Dutch coast. Wally handed the boat over to Dickens, then took up his favourite lookout position at the back of the bridge.

They had been sweeping up the route for twenty minutes when suddenly starshell began bursting overhead. The flashless cordite had concealed the origin of the enemy, but the bark of his guns now shattered the silence on the bridge of 234.

'Make to 21. "Eight Alpha",' Peter Dickens shouted to Haines, his signalman.

The shaded lamp flickered and the signal was passed to the Senior Officer of the Gunboats … *Attack!*

A convoy escort was dead ahead, less than 400 yards away. To Peter's astonishment, the two M.G.B.s turned away to starboard. *Must have some reason,* he thought, but then he watched Smyth, the third gunboat, M.G.B. 18, who clearly must have seen the signal, dart suddenly up to full speed and charge straight in towards the enemy. He swung off to starboard, firing with everything he had as he swept by, and successfully drawing much of the enemy's fire upon himself. He was a magnificent man, thought Dickens: huge in every way. With his beetling black eyebrows and his belly laugh, Smyth was entirely uninhibited.

The air was full of tracer, flying cannon splinters, smoke and starshell. Dickens and his next astern, John Perkins in M.T.B. 230, were under concentrated fire and sustaining damage, when Peter saw Smyth swing out at full speed to starboard to join his comrades, who were now also passing up the starboard wing of the enemy.

Wally, amazed at the sudden turn of events, watched as, within thirty seconds of action being joined, Smyth suddenly collided with the second M.G.B. Smyth's boat completely rode over his comrade's port quarter, the bows rearing high into the air before sliding back into the water as the second M.G.B. drew clear. Even at this distance, as Peter Dickens went 'hard over' at full speed to a reciprocal course, Wally could see that M.G.B. 18 was grievously wounded. There seemed to be an enormous hole in her bottom and she was filling rapidly.

Dickens took advantage of the confusion to lose himself, but not before being seriously savaged by the escorting flak trawlers. As he leapt ahead, away from the convoy to reform, he decided to make smoke. He leant down and turned the patent cock which he had fitted on the bridge. Using full rudder, he disappeared behind the merciful cloud of smoke from the canisters on the quarterdeck.

John Perkins began to follow his leader but, suffering intense fire, decided he would do better on the other side of the enemy, so altered course violently in the opposite direction.

Wally last saw M.T.B. 230 wheeling off to starboard, directly towards the enemy's stern. She then disappeared in smoke.

Dickens, meanwhile, maintained his three-quarter circle and came cautiously out of the smoke. To his surprise, instead of the escort being at a greater distance, the trawler was nearer than before. *I'd better discard this fixed idea in my mind,* he thought; *the convoy* must *be steering south-west, not north-east.* He quickly adjusted his deflection bar and set on left deflection. He decided to continue closing the convoy from its beam.

'Ready both,' he shouted.

Wally, his eyes smarting from the smoke, could just distinguish John Perkins in M.T.B. 230 creeping in between the escorts and the target, the supply ship. He watched 230 pause for a moment. He saw the torpedo splashes. Then she turned on her heel and roared off at full speed, clouds of smoke shielding her as she escaped from the barrage of fire she had now called down upon herself.

Wally held his breath, waiting for the torpedo hits. There was a sheet of flame, and orange and red haloes in the night. The supply ship then disintegrated with a terrible roar which rumbled around the horizon like midsummer thunder.

'God,' Wally whispered to himself. 'How terrible.'

Dickens had not heeded the explosion, his eyes intent along his firing bar.

'Two or three degrees to go, Cox'n ... let her swing ... gently ... gently ... *Stand by...*'

The sights came on:

*'Fire both!'*

Once again, the hiss as the torpedoes leapt over the bows, at the identical moment when the enemy opened fire on him, again with everything he had. In the holocaust of tracer, searchlight beams, flame and smoke, Peter was completely blinded.

'Full ahead,' he cried as he rang down his orders on the telegraphs to the engine room. 234 sprung from her firing position, leaping away like a greyhound loosed from the traps.

Wally watched with admiration the total self-control of Dickens when he realised that, after all this sacrifice and agony, he had missed with both his torpedoes. The man's face, though set in grim lines, betrayed the bitter disappointment.

'I should have stuck to my guns — she was steering *north-east*,' he said quietly. 'I set the wrong deflection. Sorry, blokes.'

Wally could see the misery in his C.O.'s face. Upon him lay the whole responsibility, the lightning thinking, the instinctive decisions; and upon him the responsibility of the killed and the wounded.

234 was charging out of the smoke again when she came upon Smyth, the bows of his M.G.B. awash and her stern in the air, her propellers threshing wildly above the surface. She was completely out of control.

'Port wheel. Slow ahead both,' Dickens commanded, picking up his megaphone.

'I could only cope by going flat out,' Smyth shouted. 'But now my forepart's flooding. Can you try to tow me?'

Dickens nodded. 'Stand by to be taken in tow, stern first.'

As the tow was being prepared in 234, starshell began bursting overhead, turning night into day. The towing hawsers went across and were secured. Then Dickens went slow ahead, but it was hopeless: M.G.B. 18 yawed uncontrollably at the end of her tow, in spite of variations in length.

'It's hopeless,' Dickens called across to Smyth. 'Stand by to abandon ship. I'll come alongside and take you off.'

'Right.'

A heavy swell was now running, so Dickens made several approaches. At each attempt men jumped across the crashing gunwales until, finally, only Smyth and his motor mechanic were left.

'Give me a few more minutes,' Smyth shouted. 'We're flooding the engine room with petrol, and I've just got to collect my C.B.s.'

Dickens shoved off for his last circuit and Smyth was about to set fire to his boat with a Verey's cartridge: a hazardous operation, as Lieutenant Christopher Dreyer found out when he blew up his stricken M.T.B. with a Verey's light.

At that moment, 234's motor mechanic popped his head up from the engine room hatch. As he was peering around, he suddenly began shouting towards his captain. 'Well, look at that, sir!' he yelled above the racket. 'That's all right, isn't it? There's them perishin' gunboats come to 'elp us!'

Dickens swung round. He was smiling wanly, for even in this catastrophe, the rivalry between the M.T.B.s and the M.G.B.s still existed. He glanced at the advancing bow waves. Then his heart missed a beat: there were *four* craft approaching. They could not be British gunboats coming to help, because there were only three left. They could only be German VP-boats. They looked huge now as they careered down upon him, 200 yards distant, all guns suddenly opening fire.

Dickens crashed 234 portside-to alongside M.G.B. 18, who had not yet begun to burn fiercely from the Verey's light Smyth had fired into the petrol-filled engine room. As the boats touched, Smyth and his motor mechanic jumped. Smyth's final gesture was to bring his C.B.s with him, all bagged up and mustered.

234 was now heading towards the advancing enemy, because Dickens had been forced to manoeuvre as dictated by

seamanship. The obvious way to draw clear of the burning M.G.B. was to turn to starboard because of the shorter arc. The turn would take longer in time, however, because 234 would be unable to turn until her stern was clear of M.G.B. 18; and also because 234's wing propellers were both right-handed. The boat turned faster to port by going ahead on the starboard propeller and with the rudders hard-a-port, because the paddlewheel effect assisted the turn, instead of retarding it, as happened when turning to starboard.

As 234 drew clear she slowly began to swing to port. In this agonising moment, Dickens found himself directly between the inferno of the blazing gunboat and the advancing enemy, who, with all guns firing, were leaping in for the kill. They were less than a hundred yards away.

Dickens was still only halfway round his turn, still trying to reach the far side of the blazing gunboat. With two crews packed on board and lying face down on the upper deck which was being raked with tracer by the enemy; with only two engines; with no gun with which to defend themselves, Peter Dickens knew that the end had come.

Wally too was now lying flat on the upper deck. He'd done all he could by dragging the wounded to the far side, away from the exposed flanks of the boat. Now, as the murderous fire swept the decks, he knew that this was the final curtain. *Kaput,* as the Hun said.

Wally glanced up at his captain. He stood there, calmly waiting for the end. Above them fluttered their battle ensign... they'd never haul down their colours, never surrender... *Dear God, let my end be quick,* Wally prayed to his Maker as he'd never prayed before.

Then suddenly, from somewhere amidships, the staccato *rap-rap-rap* of a Strip-Lewis gun began stuttering. A snaking line of green tracer spurted from between the tubes. There was a loud cheer, and then Wally saw him: the burly figure of their passenger — Petty Officer Ross, who had asked to accompany them because he owned his own personal armoury. Instantly the fire from the VP-boats went wild, most of it going high.

Peter Dickens seized this fleeting chance. In these vital seconds he managed to reach a position behind the blazing M.G.B.

The Lewis gun was pumping a stream of tracer straight at the leading VP-boat. Ross's aim was accurate, for suddenly, at 150 yards, the leading boat sheered off to port, its three consorts, in close order, following astern. They were turning with full rudder, but a couple of minutes would be needed for them to turn full circle and attack again.

234 was now shielded by the burning M.G.B. The VP-boats were blinded by the flames and by the stream of bullets from the single Lewis gun.

Dickens yanked at his telegraphs. 234 shivered, then gathered way. Wally watched the crackling skeleton of the M.G.B. slide swiftly past them. The holocaust suddenly diminished as 234 retrieved the mantle of darkness, away from the glare of battle.

'Steer west,' Dickens ordered calmly, above the roar of the engines. 'What about some hot soup, Cox'n?'

The casualties were miraculously light: no one was seriously wounded in M.T.B. 234 and only two were minor casualties from M.G.B. 18. M.T.B. 234, on her remaining two engines, proceeded slowly across the wintry sea and returned to base.

# CHAPTER 10

*The Raid on Dieppe*
*19th August 1942*

Wally Bruce was not to share in Peter Dickens's further exploits when, as Senior Officer of the Twenty-first M.T.B. Flotilla, he led his boats against the enemy with such brilliant results. Wally was sad to leave such a band of men, but the disappointment was mitigated by the pleasure of rejoining his repaired M.G.B. 336 at Portsmouth.

It was good to see Jannaway again; heartening to be greeted by his ship's company. A few days working up off the Isle of Wight and the little ship had formed up again with Nye and his First Division of the Fourteenth M.G.B. Flotilla.

During May and June of 1942, numbers of M.L.s, Chasers, M.G.B.s and destroyers were to be seen exercising with all types of landing craft. This assault fleet was dispersed in harbours along the south coast, but the personnel had been trained from the Combined Operations Headquarters at Cowes where, under the overall direction of the Chief of Combined Operations, Vice-Admiral Lord Louis Mountbatten, Captain Jock Hughes-Hallett commanded and trained his Naval Force.

Everyone along the south coast knew that a larger raid than usual was afoot. Rumours flew through the pubs: the Second Front was imminent — at any moment the British were about to land again in France to relieve the Russians from the German assault upon the eastern flanks of Europe.

All through that hot and lazy June, the ships waited near their bases: swinging at anchor in St Helen's Roads; cooped up inside Shoreham; scraping up and down the piles in Littlehampton and Newhaven. July came; slipped by. Then August...

The original raid on Dieppe, code-named *Rutter,* was planned for 7th July but the operation was postponed because of lax security. The final date was fixed for 18th August, when there was no moon and the tide was right; for this moment Captain Jock Hughes-Hallett and his Chief of Staff, Acting Captain David Luce, D.S.O., worked incessantly during those hot summer days of 1942. After every conceivable difficulty had been overcome, including a last-minute postponement due to adverse weather conditions, Captain Hughes-Hallett made the final decision. At 1930 on 19th August, he boarded his Headquarters ship, *Calpe,* a Hunt-class destroyer, in Portsmouth harbour.

Half an hour later, as the summer evening drew in, the little armada passed in perfect formation through the eastern gate of the Spithead boom defence. Operation Jubilee, the first full-scale dress rehearsal for the liberation of Europe, had begun. Those in command knew full well the terrible risks that lay ahead.

Wally stood on the bridge of M.G.B. 336. He felt proud as he glanced round the horizon to where the dark outlines of 237 vessels of this assault force steamed remorselessly towards the French coast. It was already 0030, half an hour into what might be his last day on earth. The Force was in good order after surprisingly few mishaps. In an hour's time it would be negotiating the channel which had just been swept by the Ninth and Thirteenth Minesweeping Flotillas, through a suspected enemy minefield in mid-Channel.

'Take over, Number One, please. I'm going to have a last check of the orders and snatch half an hour's shut-eye.'

Down in the subdued light of the chart table he read over for the final time the voluminous and detailed orders for Jubilee. He glanced at the track chart. So far so good. Now to refresh his memory.

The objects of the raid on Dieppe were simple. First, to relieve the Russians on the eastern front, by mounting a frontal assault upon the Nazis' Atlantic Wall. It was hoped that the enemy, because of the raid on Dieppe, would be forced to tie down considerable numbers of troops in the defence of the Low Countries and French coastlines. Second, to test the feasibility of a frontal assault upon a defended enemy coastline, so that, when the time was ripe for a return to Europe, there could be no chance of failure. Third, since the miracle of Dunkirk, the Canadian Army in Britain had been equipped and were now trained to a high standard of efficiency. These magnificent troops were naturally becoming restive and were beginning to wonder whether the lines *They also serve who only stand and wait* were true. This major raid which included the landing of tanks from assault craft, would provide the challenge for which these fire-eating Canadians hankered.

Wally flipped over the foolscap sheets. *Assault Section*: Here it was, clearly set out.

There were to be four major assault groups, each with its own objective. The failure of any group would jeopardise the success of the others in their attack upon this French port which lay at the mouth of the River d'Arques.

Number Three Commando, under the command of Lieutenant-Colonel J. F. Durnford-Slater, D.S.O., was to land on Yellow 1 and Yellow 2 Beaches, on either side of the Goebbels Battery, which was to be destroyed. These commandos were to be put ashore by the craft of Group 5 under the general command of Commander D. B. Wyburd, R.N.

Four miles to the west of Berneval, on the eastward headland overlooking Dieppe, Rommel Battery dominated the scene at the village of Puits. The task of the Royal Regiment of Canada was to land on Blue Beach, below the eastern headland, and then to immobilise the Rommel 4-gun battery by a frontal assault, combined with a cutting-out attack from the rear. The regiment was to be transported by L.S.I.s (Landing Ship Infantry) *Queen Emma, Princess Astrid* and *Duke of Wellington,* until the lowering position was reached ten miles offshore. The 'Royals' would then be transferred to the landing craft under the command of Lieutenant-Commander H.W. Goulding. The success of this landing at Puits was vital to the whole operation.

On the western flanks of Dieppe lay four objectives: the silencing of the Hess Battery which, with its six 5.9-inch guns between the villages of Vasterival and Varengeville, dominated the foreshore; the capture of the German Army Headquarters at Pourville; the neutralising of the dominating position of Quatre Vents Farm; and the destruction of the nearby radar station.

The Hess Battery was to be silenced by Lord Lovat, No. 4 Commando of 250 men, who were to be landed by *Prince Albert*'s landing craft under the command of Lieutenant-Commander H. Mulleneux. These troops would leap ashore on either side of Hess Battery, at Orange Beach 1 on the eastern side of La Saane River; and at Orange Beach 2, between the villages of Vasterival and Varengeville.

Further objectives at Pourville were to be achieved by the South Saskatchewan Regiment which would be landed on

Green Beach by the assault craft under the command of Commander R. M. Prior, from L.S.J.s *Princess Beatrix* and *Invicta*. Half an hour later, the Cameron Highlanders of Canada were to land and pass through the South Saskatchewan in order to advance swiftly inland to destroy the airfield at St Aubin. They were then to link up with the tanks which, having been landed on Red Beach, would be fanning inland to the assumed German Divisional Headquarters at Arques-la-Bataille. They were to destroy the Hitler Battery which was sited close to these Headquarters.

The frontal assault was to take place close westward of the western mole, and immediately beneath the Dieppe esplanade. The Royal Hamilton Light Infantry from L.S.L *Glengyle*'s landing craft, under the command of Lieutenant-Commander C. W. McMullen, would be put ashore on White Beach.

Immediately to the east of White Beach, and close to the western mole, was Red Beach. Here was the vital, main beach, where the Fourteenth Canadian Tank Battalion of the Calgary Regiment, transported from England in Landing Craft Tanks, was to land. Red Beach was to be attacked and secured by the men of the Canadian Essex Scottish, who, once the tanks had broken out of the beachhead, were to control the town of Dieppe. The Essex Scottish would be landed from *Prince Charles*'s and *Prince Leopold*'s landing craft, under the command of Commander G. T. Lambert. This landing was to be backed up by the gunfire of the Hunt destroyers *Berkeley, Bleasdale, Garth* and *Albrighton* and by the cannon-firing fighters of the R.A.F., which would also blanket the eastern headland with smoke.

Waiting in the deep field in their own L.C.P.s, which had made the passage from England, were the Fusiliers Mont Royal. They were to act as the Floating Reserve.

Finally, as part of the operation, a cutting-out expedition under the command of Commander R. E. D. Ryder, of the St Nazaire raid fame, was to force its way into Dieppe Harbour where, with the support of the Chasers, the shipping and dock installations were to be attacked. This task was to be performed by men of the Royal Marine Commando, commanded by Lieutenant-Colonel J. R. P. Phillipps.

Wally sighed with relief as he finished reading the orders. He smiled to himself as he remembered the secret instructions he had been given: at 1110 precisely, he was to take 336 under cover of smoke into Orange Beach 1, where the withdrawal would have started. In the confusion several agents would be waiting to be taken off. They were to be picked up from the foreshore at the western entrance to the fishing village of Varengeville. One of them, a woman, would be wearing a green raincoat.

Wally yawned as he switched off the chart table light. At least he would have something to do. He suddenly felt happier, with an inner warmth: perhaps Suzanne might be there. She had known all along. She had asked the authorities for him, hadn't she?

He discarded the dream and stretched out on the settee.

Captain Hughes-Hallett felt reasonably satisfied as he stood on *Calpe*'s bridge. His whole force had safely, though excitingly, negotiated the swept channels, in spite of L.S.I. *Queen Emma* taking the eastern instead of the western route, and in spite of other minor complications. The L.S.I.s had lowered their L.C.P.s within three minutes of schedule, and now, at 0345, all the assault groups were on their way to the beaches as planned; with only seven miles to go, they should be landing on time an hour before sunrise. Surprise had been achieved so far, and he felt confident, having told all his Commanding Officers to remain concealed and to avoid trouble should the enemy be encountered.

'Starshell, red four-o, sir,' the port lookout cried suddenly. Hughes-Hallett picked up his binoculars. 'Talk of the devil,' he swore under his breath. Perhaps it was merely the diversionary attacks of M.G.B.s 6, 7 and 9 off Boulogne? The gunfire and starshell, though, were exactly where Wyburd in Group 5 should be... but the two Hunts, *Ślązak* (under the Polish Senior Officer) and *Brocklesby* (under Pumphrey) were there, covering Group 5, so all should be well.

Hughes-Hallett conferred with his colleague, Major General Roberts, the Military Commander. Should they call off the whole operation? Already the R.A.F. squadrons would be taking off; already the L.C.P.s were on their way into the landings. Hughes-Hallett felt again the almost unbearable weight of responsibility. The enemy would probably think that the action was a normal convoy battle: the D'Ailly lighthouse was continuing to flash in groups of three, as if the enemy was expecting a convoy to pass. He made his decision: the assault would be unleashed according to plan.

At 0510, R.A.F. Bostons attacked the eastern headland above Yellow Beach, where they laid protective smoke. *Calpe* now lay stopped, about a mile off the beaches. The Naval Force Commander directed operations from her bridge, below which a special Operations Room had been constructed, and from whence the Combined Staffs attempted to control events. The enemy was reacting swiftly, and signals began pouring into the Signals Distribution Office. *Calpe* had, therefore, because of the vital importance of communications and the sensitivity of the wireless gear, been forbidden to use her 4-inch guns. The air was alive with enemy aircraft.

Wyburd from Group 5 was now aboard *Calpe*. He had reported the failure of their landings when two bloodstained soldiers were hauled on board. They had landed from the L.C.P.s on Yellow Beach (1) at Berneval. The Goebbels Battery above the village had held its fire until the few soldiers of No. 3 Commando had swarmed on to the beach. German troops then plastered the beach with grenades hurled down from the cliff top, and then, as the Commandos rushed the cliff, the Goebbels Battery opened up on the beach and on the L.C.P.s lying offshore. None of the troops succeeded in reaching their objective. The entire force was wiped out, either mown down where they landed or captured later.

At Yellow Beach (2), L.C.P. 15 enjoyed the distinction of making a solitary landing. At 0445, five minutes before zero hour, she put ashore the Headquarters party of No. 6 Troop. There was surprisingly little opposition and by 0530, in spite of no proper equipment, Major Young and his party reached the cliff top at the identical moment when the R.A.F. began its attack on Goebbels Battery.

Young and his men succeeded in reaching a point within two hundred yards of these enormous guns. They were so close that the German guns could not depress sufficiently. From this cornfield, having been helped by the French villagers, Young's men sniped continually at the enemy gunners through the open gun ports at the rear of the German emplacements. 'It was alarming,' Major Young said later. 'If you put your hand up, you felt as if it would be cut off by a 6-inch shell.' With its machine guns and rifles, this remarkable contingent kept Goebbels Battery quiet for two hours. When they ran out of ammunition, Young returned with his men to Yellow Beach (2) where they sheltered at the foot of the cliffs beneath the

German guns until L.C.P. 15, at her second attempt, succeeded in taking them off.

Lieutenant-Commander Mulleneux, commanding the landing craft for the assault on Orange Beach, stood alongside Bobby Nye in M.G.B. 312 who, together with Lieutenant Peter Scott in Steam Gun Boat 9, was escorting the landing craft into Orange Beach (1) and (2). The 250 men from No. 4 Commando had been forced to alter course to avoid an enemy eastbound convoy, but they had split up and landed on time. Wally Bruce in 336 brought up the rear and covered the seaward flank, in case the remnants of the convoy turned back to investigate.

At Orange Beach (1), the Irish Guards landed as the R.A.F. fighters began blasting Hess Battery on the hill above Varengeville. Aided by enemy bilingual notices drawing attention to landmines, the troops slipped through the village and crept up on the battery through a wood. The 2-inch mortar was set up and, with its third shot, it exploded the German's ready-use stock of ammunition.

A blinding flash, a gigantic explosion, and then — as the guns became silent — the Commandos heard the screams and cries of the German wounded. The Commandos continued sniping with their Brens at the enemy fire-fighters and then, after silencing all the surrounding machine-gun nests, the Guards withdrew to the beach. Moments later, Lord Lovat's party, who had successfully landed at Orange (2), had wiped out with Tommy guns thirty-five Germans who were forming up to counter-attack the Irish Guards.

At 0625, as the R.A.F. fighters made another low-level air attack, Lord Lovat and his men charged Hess Battery and took it at the point of the bayonet. They blew up the guns, killed thirty of the crews and took four prisoners. They then withdrew to the beach and waited for re-embarkation.

At 0730, in spite of sniping from the cliff top, the troops of No. 4 Commando began wading out to the L.C.P.s and three extra L.C.A.s. Up to their necks in water, for the beach shelved very gradually and the tide was now ebbing fast, all these troops were taken off by 0815. Two officers and nine men were killed and thirteen men were missing. 'This landing,' said Captain Hughes-Hallett, 'was a copybook action. Lord Lovat kept me continually informed.'

After evacuating No. 4 Commando, Bobby Nye in M.G.B. 312 and Peter Scott in S.G.B. 9 spent the next few hours laying smoke off the beaches and picking up ditched airmen. At 0615, Scott told S.G.B. 8 to take station astern. Together they steamed off on a sweep, fifteen miles to the westward in accordance with previous orders; they were to give warning of the five T-class torpedo boats if they emerged from Cherbourg.

As the two S.G.B.s left the relative safety of the R.A.F. umbrella, a sense of false security descended upon the two boats. The French cliffs shone in the early morning sunlight; the woods and fields were a fresh green. Scott failed to realise that some cliff-watchers must already have telephoned for the Luftwaffe to sink these two impertinent British ships.

Seconds later the S.G.B.s were swooped upon by two ME 109s. S.G.B. 9 was near-missed, but her boilers were shaken up and lost their vacuum. To his horror, Scott realised that he was stopped and out of action, a sitting duck. 'Griff' (Lieutenant I. R. Griffiths, R.N.) in S.G.B. 8 bumped alongside and took Scott in tow. Together, entirely unprotected, the two S.G.B.s began limping back at 7 knots towards Dieppe. Then at 0755, the Engineer Officer reported that the boiler was functioning again. With a sigh of relief S.G.B. 9 increased gradually to 30 knots. A signal had just come in reporting that E-boats had ventured out from Boulogne. This was more in the S.G.B.s' line of business.

Events were deteriorating at Blue Beach. Lieutenant-Commander Goulding, R.N.R., by making his landfall on the green light at the end of the eastern mole, had been forced to make a dog-leg before touching down on Blue Beach at Puits. This action produced two serious results: first, he landed sixteen minutes late; second, as daylight was breaking, he passed so close to the beach that his force suffered serious damage. The landing craft succeeded in landing their troops of the Royal Regiment of Canada, but, when the soldiers were 100 yards off the beach and clear of the smoke laid by the R.A.F., they came under murderous and accurate fire from Rommel Battery on the cliff top. When they reached the lofty sea wall, which ran along the beach fifty yards from the water's edge, they were pinned down on either flank by enfilading fire.

In spite of reinforcements from further waves of the L.C.A.s, who were being covered by L.C.S.s 25 and 28, firing at point-blank range against the indestructible pillboxes, the troops could make no headway against such withering fire. There could only be one result: *The troops never succeeded in getting beyond the sea wall, where they were pinned down by steadily increasing fire, until all but a few men, who escaped by swimming, were either killed or captured.* 24 officers and 459 men were killed, wounded or missing out of 27 officers and 516 men who embarked. The vital attack at Puits had failed utterly.

The South Saskatchewans landed on Green Beach on time. They overcame heavy machine gun and A.A. fire, and pressed on towards their objectives. The German Headquarters in Pourville were overrun; the radar station was surrounded, but not captured, through lack of mortar and artillery support. The farm at Quatre Vents was closely invested but, in spite of tenacious efforts, this heavily defended position was not taken before the Saskatchewans were finally ordered to withdraw.

The Queen's Own Cameron Highlanders of Canada landed half an hour late, under Commander H. C. McClintock. Though the soldiers' Commanding Officer, Lieutenant-Colonel A. S. Gosling, was killed as he jumped ashore, they managed to move up the Scie river towards St Aubin airfield. They were unable, however, to take the vital bridge. Pinned down, they waited in vain for the tanks from Red and White Beaches to arrive. If the armour did not appear soon, time would run out and they would be forced to retire. What *had* happened to the tanks?

# CHAPTER 11

*The Final Sacrifice*
*19th August 1942*

The main assault at White and Red Beaches was against the Dieppe sea front itself, an esplanade which stretched for 1,700 yards and which was backed by the sea wall, boulevards and gardens. At 0512, the supporting destroyers opened fire on this sea front. Then the R.A.F. went in, blasting all the defences in sight.

The landing craft, led by M.G.B. 326 and M.L. 291 beached at 0523, only three minutes late. They suffered only slight opposition because the enemy was still reeling from the effects of the destroyer's bombardment. The Royal Hamiltons, instead of advancing rapidly, lost precious minutes whilst forming up beneath the protection of the sea wall. This momentary delay sealed their fate, for by the time they began to scale the wall the Germans had recovered: a murderous fire was poured from enfilading gun positions in the east cliff upon White and Red Beaches. These guns could not be detected even at close range, until they fired, so they were not easily silenced by the Hamiltons. The troops could neither hold the beach nor advance, caught as they were in this terrible crossfire and halted by the thick barbed-wire entanglements.

The tanks fared even worse at Red Beach. Though twenty-eight out of thirty managed to lumber ashore from the L.C.T.s, two being 'drowned', they soon became bogged down by the shingle on the beach. They ranged slowly up and down, but could render little aid. Instead, they became sitting targets for the German gunners firing from the eastern headland. Fifteen tanks succeeded in reaching the promenade, but because the exits to the streets were blocked they were forced to return forlornly to the beach.

The first and second waves of L.C.T.s had suffered heavily and, when *Fernie* realised the seriousness of the situation ashore, it was decided not to send in the third and fourth waves.

During these tragic moments, L.C.F. (L) 2 was sunk whilst lending support at point-blank range. *Locust* could not bombard effectively because of the confused situation ashore but, nevertheless, she approached the harbour entrance and engaged the Rommel Battery on the east cliff with her 4-inch gun. She was then badly hit, suffering severe casualties, and was forced to retire.

The destroyers, too, dashed in to help. *Albrighton* silenced an A.A. battery above Pourville; *Bleasdale* took on a battery 100 yards to the east of Dieppe but could not silence it; *Garth* bombarded the east cliff. Nevertheless, the lighter guns of the destroyers were ineffective against the heavy German batteries.

*Throughout this period,* wrote Captain Hughes-Hallett afterwards, *enemy fire from the shore steadily increased, and the destroyers were forced constantly to shift their positions, in order to avoid damage and keep under cover of smoke… H.M.S.* Calpe, *during most of this period, must have resembled a Fleet Flagship on regatta day, as there were seldom less than from six to ten craft alongside. They came to transfer wounded, bring reports or receive instructions, and their presence was often an embarrassment to the Commanding Officer when he wished to manoeuvre to avoid gunfire. My general impression during this phase was a feeling of inability to give the troops effective support. The military situation was completely obscure, and the large quantities of smoke drifting inshore made it impossible to see what was happening.*

Seldom has great gallantry been so ill rewarded. At about 0650, Wyburd came aboard *Calpe* to report the dismal news from Blue Beach. Captain Hughes-Hallett went below to see Major General Roberts in the Operations Room.

Against Captain Hughes-Hallett's advice, the Floating Reserve of the French Canadians, Les Fusiliers Mont Royals, were sent into Red Beach. They were trapped on the beach and were mown down when they landed. By noon, 288 of them — 100 of them wounded — were forced to surrender.

Captain Hughes-Hallett was by now considering advancing the time of withdrawal. He could tempt fate no longer. From the bridge of *Calpe,* he was soon to watch *Brocklesby* go aground by the stern: she had approached too close to the beach in order to lend support to bombardment. Her engines were temporarily out of action but, within 300 yards of the beach, it was remarkable how fast her engine-room staff could work. Within three minutes she was repaired. Her screws threshed and, with a shudder, she was off and retiring fast to the northward. *Garth*, too, was virtually useless, having run out of 4-inch ammunition. And now, very shortly, the cutting-out expedition was due to enter the harbour, to be carried in by the Chasers of Group 13. Hughes-Hallett asked Ryder for his opinion. 'It would be madness,' was the reply.

'Abandon the cutting-out expedition,' Hughes-Hallett commanded. 'The Royal Marine Commando is to be put at the disposal of the Military Force Commanders.'

Thus it was that the Royal Marine Commando, consisting of 18 officers and 352 men, under the command of Lieutenant-Colonel J.R.P. Phillipps, R.M., was sent in to White Beach. Transhipping from *Locust* and the Chasers, the Royal Marines boarded seven L.C.A.s and L.C.M.s from the boat pool. Then, escorted by three Chasers on either flank, the Royal Marines moved in towards White Beach through the smoke.

When they emerged the scene was one of complete hopelessness. *It was not long before I realised,* wrote Lieutenant Malcolm Buist, R.N., Senior Officer of the Chasers, *that this landing was to be a sea-parallel of The Charge of the Light Brigade.*

At that moment, fire was opened up at 4,000 yards from the shore, the range decreasing as the Chasers advanced. The firing emanated from the eastern cliff and from the mole, and now machine-gun and rifle fire had joined in. At this point the Chasers were running out of water and were forced to turn or they would have grounded.

Lieutenant E. G. Egerton, R.N., was Captain of Chaser 13. As he turned his ship, she was hit in the wheelhouse by a heavy shell. Egerton and his signalman, Gillespie, were standing directly above on the bridge. Gillespie's leg was severed below the knee, while his Captain was mortally wounded. Egerton calmly carried on; holding on to the voicepipe for support, he extricated his ship from her perilous predicament. As he collapsed from loss of blood, he turned to one of his lookouts: 'Please ask the First Lieutenant to relieve me.' They took him below to his cabin where they laid him on his bunk. When they removed his boots, they were full of his life-blood. 'Egg' had saved his ship and the men of whom he was so proud: his 'braves', as he always called them.

The assault craft, with Lieutenant-Colonel Phillipps in the van, pressed on towards the beach. As they emerged from the smoke, it was obvious to Phillipps that it was suicidal and pointless to continue. There was not a second to be lost.

Phillipps donned a pair of white gloves, so that his hands would be visible. He jumped on to the foredeck of his landing craft, where he could more easily be seen by those following.

In those few seconds he signalled to the craft following astern to put about and head for the shelter of the smoke and the open sea. Then he was cut down by a hail of fire. He fell, mortally wounded, but he had saved 200 of his men from certain death.

Buist then signalled to the Naval Force Commander that the position on Red and White Beaches was out of control.

In *Calpe*, Captain Hughes-Hallett had no time to blame himself for allowing the Royal Marine Commando to be used. The air battle — the greatest and most concentrated of the war — raged about him and his hard-pressed armada.

The R.A.F.'s response was magnificent. Wing Commander Sprott, the Visual Director — a man of the highest competence — had been appointed to *Calpe* by Air Vice-Marshal Leigh-Mallory. Working alongside Hughes-Hallett, Sprott would take over the individual direction of his fighters.

'To Uxbridge,' he would command over the R/T. 'I will take Red Fighter Five — NOW.'

An immediate reply would follow: 'From Uxbridge: Red Fighter Five, act under *Calpe*.'

Then Sprott: 'Red Fighter Five: fly towards Puits and shoot up Dornier attacking destroyer *Fernie*.' The results were remarkable, particularly when the enemy bombers were close.

The Germans had reacted slowly in the air, but then they threw in everything they could muster in northern France, including trainee pilots in their training bombers. Shortly before 0900, a German pilot was brought before Hughes-Hallett, during one of those ominous lulls which developed.

'Beg pardon, sir, but I believe you're the Senior Naval Officer?' a sailor asked him.

'Yes,' said Hughes-Hallett.

'There's a young gent waiting to speak to you, sir.'

'What?'

'I think he's a German, sir.'

A youth with fair curly hair stepped forward, clicked his heels and bowed. He was dressed in flying kit. 'I'm Unterleutnant Schmitt, and I have the honour of declaring myself your prisoner,' he said in good English.

'How on earth did you get here?'

'Very simple, sir,' the pilot said. 'I came down in my parachute a hundred yards away from your ship. She was stopped. I swam. Your sailors helped me on board. I have been waiting here until you were free.'

'But you're completely dry,' Commander Luce, who was standing close to Hughes-Hallett, interposed. 'How did you dry yourself?'

'The sun.' The pilot clicked his heels.

'You're lucky,' Luce said.

There was an angry outburst from the Unterleutnant:

'You call me lucky, sir? You need never worry again about the Luftwaffe. None of us will ever have confidence in our commanders since this morning. Look at the time… not yet nine o'clock.

'I was given leave until noon today. We were all given this morning off, all of us stationed at Abbeville; I don't care if I do break all the rules by telling you this. Last night I went to the pictures with a friend. Then we took rooms for the night and I told the military police of our whereabouts, just as the orders say.' The young man was a picture of injured pride. 'Then at five-thirty this morning,' he continued, 'a military policeman, NOT an officer, actually touched me with his hand. "You are to go back to your station at once," the policeman said. "Don't argue. There's a car waiting." When I reached the station the Commandant was waiting at the gate. "Fly to Dieppe," he said.

'I took off at dawn and then looked for Abbeville. Suddenly I was surrounded by hundreds of Spitfires. I just had time to fire one burst. My friend, who had no ammunition, was shot down in flames. Then they got me. No, sir,' he concluded, 'this is not my lucky day.'

Luce burst out laughing, but the pilot continued:

'Before I was called up I was a medical student for five years. Is it correct for me to help the wounded?'

'Yes,' said Hughes-Hallett.

The man was a tremendous help with the wounded, and when it was all over the Naval Force Commander asked the King to mention the German in dispatches.

At ten o'clock, Captain Hughes-Hallett was convinced that the withdrawal should be advanced, but Major General Roberts insisted that it should take place as planned at 1100: there would not be time to reorganise the troops or to warn the R.A.F.

Hughes-Hallett then told McClintock to reorganise the L.C.A.s and L.C.M.s and to take them in at 1100 to the beaches where they had originally landed. 'The L.C.T.s are too big under these circumstances,' the Captain said. 'You are to bring off personnel only. I'll signal the destroyers to form a line of bearing of 050 degrees. They will cover you with the L.C.F.s and give you maximum support.'

So, at 1100, began the immensely difficult task of a reorganised withdrawal. In spite of incredible efforts by the small ships and by the troops ashore, the rearguard had to be left ashore on Green Beach.

On Red and White Beaches the sacrifice of ships and men was even worse. Commander McClintock, unable to find *Calpe,* had signalled the Naval Force Commander that no further evacuation was possible from White and Red Beaches.

Major General Roberts asked for one final effort to bring off more troops, so Hughes-Hallett signalled: *If no further evacuation possible, withdraw.*

Unfortunately the signal was repeated to McClintock without the word 'if', so he withdrew with all the landing craft within sight of him, without apparently having been in again to the beaches. By this time, showing utter contempt for danger, the crews of the landing craft had brought off 400 men from Red and White Beaches. On all these beaches desperate men tried to rush the mercy craft, sinking some of them by over-loading. Other troops, risking all, swam out to sea, desperately waiting to be picked up. Then, slowly, the landing craft retreated. The fallen figures remaining on the beach never moved.

At 1240, the Naval Force Commander took *Calpe* inshore for his final inspection. She opened fire as she dashed through the smoke towards Green Beach, which seemed very close.

At nine cables from the shore she came under heavy fire. Hughes-Hallett saw that he could control nothing, except by questioning the landing craft as they came out. It appeared impossible to bring off any more troops, so he began to take *Calpe* out to seaward. As he did so, he saw *Locust,* a monitor of shallow draught, bombarding the eastern cliff. He steamed towards her, intending to ask Ryder, who was on board, for his advice as to whether *Locust* should make one final attempt to bring off the last of the troops.

At this moment, Major General Roberts came on to the bridge, his face ashen grey with fatigue and despair.

'They're surrendering,' he said. 'There's no point in going on.'

When *Calpe* made the signal for evacuation, she ordered the destroyers to close and make smoke. Air attacks became continuous and one bomb struck *Berkeley*, who was bombarding houses behind White Beach. Her back was broken beneath the bridge and she began to sink. S.G.B. 8 rushed alongside to take off her company. Colonel Hillsinger, an American, who had his legs cut off by the explosion, gallantly remained behind on *Berkeley*'s bridge when she was finally torpedoed and sunk by *Albrighton*.

An L.C.T. had broken down a mile from shore. Many L.C.A.s, when coming out, dumped their wounded aboard the L.C.T. before going in again for further loads. The L.C.T., however, at the last moment using her initiative, went in and fully loaded for a last effort to bring off the few remaining troops. She was sunk then, with large numbers on board, only half a mile from the beach.

Then, in spite of German ruses to tempt the L.C.A.s inshore, the evacuation was abandoned: only about 368 men had been evacuated from Red and White Beaches.

On the way out, one of Wing Commander Sprott's assistants clutched Hughes-Hallett's shoulder.

'Could you possibly pick up that pilot in the water over there?' he pleaded.

'No. I daren't risk *Calpe* with all these men and wounded on board,' the Captain replied brusquely.

'But he's my best friend.'

Hughes-Hallett hesitated. Then he turned to his Yeoman of Signals. 'Make *Disregard my movements*, Yeoman.'

David Luce, the Chief of Staff, spoke up. 'If you do that, sir, you'll lose the ship once you are separated from the fighter cover. All the enemy aircraft will pounce on you.'

Hughes-Hallett stuck to his decision, but Luce was almost proved right. Once *Calpe* was alone and streaking for the airman in the water, hordes of Junkers 87s screamed out of the sky. *Calpe* was accurately bombed and smothered by a succession of near misses, many soldiers being killed on the upper deck. The Ready-Use ammunition locker at the centre gun caught fire and six sailors, their clothes alight, jumped into the sea to extinguish the flames.

Peter Scott, who was not far away in S.G.B. 9, saw *Calpe* disappear in the mountainous plumes of the bomb splashes. He turned to his signalman.

'Make a signal, *Calpe sunk*,' he said.

'Don't do that, sir,' his First Lieutenant interrupted. 'Her bow wave's coming through.'

And there, emerging from the drifting spray of the splashes, came *Calpe*'s bows. Peter Scott turned immediately to pick up the six sailors. Then, after a long search, he finally sighted the R.A.F. pilot.

Hughes-Hallett, streaking back to the cover of the Spitfire umbrella, had learnt his lesson. His action, however, achieved one good result: the R.A.F. tended later to forgive the Royal Navy for the several aircraft which they had shot down in error.

Whilst the evacuation was being completed, an unobserved final act was taking place at Varengeville. Wally Bruce, under cover of the drifting smoke, had seized his opportunity and was taking M.G.B. 336 in towards the harbour mouth at full speed. Hess Battery was strangely silent, and only desultory firing was being directed at the speeding gunboat. As Wally swept through the harbour entrance, he caught sight of two figures crouching behind a hut on the breakwater. One was taller than the other, who was dressed in a green raincoat.

He eased down and manoeuvred M.G.B. 336 gently alongside the piles of the breakwater, the seamen for'd holding on with grappling irons. The two figures stood above him but, as they prepared to jump, a group of German soldiers began running down the quay, machine pistols spraying the road.

'Jump, Suzanne!' the Frenchman cried.

336's Oerlikon opened up. The advancing soldiers checked in their stride. The Frenchman turned to face his pursuers. He deliberately placed himself between the enemy and his smaller comrade as a shield. He drew a small pistol and began firing towards his foe, now less than fifty yards away.

'Jump, for God's sake, jump!' Wally yelled.

The woman leapt into the waiting arms beneath her.

The German weapons opened up again. The Frenchman jerked, then sank slowly to his knees. As he fell, he turned towards the boat, blood pouring from his face. *'Vive la France!'* Gilbert Fragonard was shouting. *'Vive, vive la France…'*

As 336 threshed astern, Wally saw the valiant Fragonard, still on one knee, firing from the hip. For those precious seconds, the Germans halted once again. As the gunboat turned, Fragonard collapsed, his body slumping to the quay.

Wally opened up the throttles. Then M.G.B. 336, raking the quayside with her Rolls gun as she swept out of the harbour, escaped to the open sea.

# EPILOGUE

The remnants of the forces which took part in the Dieppe Raid finally reached the safety of their home ports of Portsmouth and Newhaven. The Allied losses were grievous: 1,179 officers and men had given their lives. 4,260 were casualties from all causes: killed, wounded, missing, and prisoners of war.

One truth is certain: their sacrifice was not in vain. The Dieppe Raid taught the Allies the lessons which had to be learnt before the attempt could be made for the final assault to open the Second Front in Europe. Almost two years later the Normandy landings were to take place. Without the lessons learnt at Dieppe, D-Day, 6th June 1944, might have heralded the greatest military disaster in history.

The Dieppe Raid can best be summed up by quoting the words of Admiral of the Fleet, The Earl Mountbatten of Burma, who was Chief of Combined Operations. At the Commemoration of the 25th Anniversary of the Dieppe Raid, he spoke to the Frenchmen and Allies assembled in Dieppe on 19th August 1967:

It is generally acknowledged that the casualties among the vast assault force that landed in Normandy in 1944 were far lighter than anyone could have hoped for in 1942; and this can be directly attributed to the heavy casualties Britain suffered in the infinitely smaller force that landed at Dieppe. Those gallant men who gave their lives at Dieppe, by their supreme sacrifice, gave to the Allies the priceless secret of victory in the subsequent assaults.

'Years ago, one of our greatest Generals paid a tribute to his officers by saying that his battles were won on the playing fields of Eton. I have no doubt that the Battle of Normandy was won on the beaches of Dieppe. For every one man who died at Dieppe in 1942, *at least ten or more must have been spared in Normandy in* 1944.

'France owes her successful liberation to a large extent to the vital lessons which we learnt at Dieppe. The name of Dieppe will therefore live forever in the history of France and the Allies.'

# A NOTE TO THE READER

Dear Reader,

If you have enjoyed the novel enough to leave a review on **Amazon** and **Goodreads**, then we would be truly grateful.

**Sapere Books** is an exciting new publisher of brilliant fiction and popular history.

To find out more about our latest releases and our monthly bargain books visit our website: **saperebooks.com**